beautiful
boys

Francesca Lia Block

beautiful boys

■ HARPERCOLLINS*PUBLISHERS*

Library of Congress Cataloging-in-Publication Data is available.

ISBN 0-06-059435-7 (pbk.)

Typography by Alicia Mikles

1 2 3 4 5 6 7 8 9 10

First Edition

beautiful boys

beautiful boys

missing
angel juan

Angel Juan and I walk through a funky green fog. It smells like hamburgers and jasmine. We don't see anybody, not even a shadow behind a curtain in the tall houses. Like the fog swirled in through all the windows, down the halls, up the staircases, into the bedrooms and took everybody away. Then fog beasties breathed clouds onto the mirrors, checked out the bookshelves, sniffed at the refrigerator—whispering. We hear one playing drums in a room in a tower.

Angel Juan stops to listen, slinking his shoulders to the beat. "Not as good as you," he says.

I play an imaginary drum with imaginary sticks. I am writing a new song for him in my head.

He sees something on the other side of a wall and

3

picks me up. I feel his arms hard against the bottom of my ribs. Jungle garden. Water rushes. Dark house. Bright window. A piano with the head of Miss Nefertiti-ti on top.

"You look like her," he says. "Your eyes and your skinny flower-stem neck."

"But she doesn't have my snarl-ball hair or my curly toes." My toes curl like cashew nuts.

He puts me down and messes up my messy hair the way he used to do when we were little kids. Before he ever kissed me.

A black cat with a question-mark tail follows us for blocks. He has fur just like Angel Juan's hair. Angel Juan crouches down to stroke him and I stroke Angel Juan. We are all three electric in the fog. The cat keeps following us. I hear him wailing for a long time after he disappears into the wet cloud air. Angel Juan has one arm around me and is holding my inside hand with his outside hand. It is our brother grip. We are bound together. My outside hand is at his skinny hips, quick and sleeky-sleek like a cat's hips. I could put one finger into the change pocket of his black Levi's.

I want to take his photograph with his hand at the

cat's throat, his eyes closed, feeling the purr in his fingers. I want to take his picture naked in the fog.

The shiny brown St. John's bread pods crack open under our feet and their cocoa smell makes me dizzy and hungry.

Then Angel Juan stops walking. It's so quiet. Nothing moves. There's a shiver in the branches like a cat's spine when you stroke it. The green druggy fog.

I remember the first time he ever kissed me. I mean really kissed me. We had just finished a gig with our band The Goat Guys and he put his hands on my shoulders. His hair was slicked back and it gleamed, his lips were tangy and his fingers were callusy and we were both so sweaty that we stuck together. Our eyelashes brushed like they would weave together by themselves turning us into one wild thing.

I say, "I think I missed you before I met you even."

"Witch Baby," he says. He never calls me that. Niña Bruja or Baby or Lamb but never Witch Baby. I start to feel a little sick to my stomach. Queased out. Angel Juan's eyes look different. Like somebody else's eyes stuck in his head. Why did I say that about missing him? I never say clutchy stuff like that.

"I'm going to New York."

New York. We were going to go there. We were going to play music on the street. What is he saying? He just told me I looked like Nefertiti. He just had his arms around me in our brother grip.

"You're always taking pictures of me and writing songs for me but that's not me. That's who you make up. And in the band. I feel like I'm just backing up the rest of you. I've got to play my own music."

"Just go do it with her," I say.

"There's no her. I don't even feel like sex at all. Nothing feels safe."

For the last few weeks we've been snuggling but that's about it. I've been telling myself it's just because Angel Juan's been tired from working so much at the restaurant.

"But we've only ever been with us."

"Do we want to be together just because we think it's safer? I need to know about the world. I need to know me."

Safer? I've never even thought of that.

My heart is like a teacup covered with hairline cracks. I feel like I have to walk real carefully so it won't get shaken and just all shatter and break.

But I start to run anyway. I run and run into the fog before Angel Juan can go away.

By the time I get back to the house with the antique windows, I feel the jagged teacup chips cutting me up. I go into the dark garden shed. The doglet Tiki-Tee who has soul-eyes like Angel Juan's and likes to cuddle in the bend of my knees at night whimpers and skulks away when he sees me. Skulkster dog. I must look like a beastly beast with a cracked teacup for a heart. I lie on the floor listening for the broken sound inside like when you shake your thermos that fell on the cement.

We used to lie here hugging with a balloon between us. Angel Juan's body floating on the balloon, his body shining through its skin. Then the balloon popped and we giggled and screamed falling into each other, all the sadness inside of us gone into the air.

All over the walls are pictures I took of Angel Juan. Angel Juan plays his bass—eyelash-shadow, mouth-pout, knee-swoon. Angel Juan kisses the sky. Angel Juan the blur does hip-hop moves. There's even one of us together in Joshua Tree standing on either side of our cactus Sunbear. It's like Sunbear's our kid or something. We're holding hands behind him. You can see our grins under our suede desert hats and our skinny legs in hiking boots. I never let anybody take my picture unless it's Angel Juan or I'm with Angel Juan. If you saw this picture you'd probably think that Angel Juan Perez and Witch Baby Secret Agent Wigg Bat will be together forever. They will build an adobe house with a bright-yellow door in a desert oasis and play music with their friends all night while the coyotes howl at the moon. That's what you'd think. You'd never think that Angel Juan would go away.

That's why I like photographs.

And that's why I hate photographs.

I want to smash the lens of my camera. I want to smash everything.

When I feel like this I play my drums. But I don't want to play my drums. I want to smash my drums. So I'll never write or play another song for Angel Juan. "Angel Boy," "Funky Desert Heaven," "Cannibal Love." I wish I could smash the songs and the feelings the way you smash a camera lens or put your fist through the skin of a drum.

Some native Americans believe that the drum is the heart of the universe. What happens to the rest of something when you smash its heart?

Then I hear a noise outside and my heart starts going to the beat of "Cannibal Love." It's him. It's him. Him. Him. Him. Hymn.

"Witch Baby," he whispers on the other side of the door. I don't say anything.

"I still love you," he says. "I'm sorry." His voice sounds different, like somebody else is inside of him using his voice.

I don't move. It's hard to breathe. Afraid the broken pieces cutting.

"Let me in," he says. "Please. I leave tomorrow."

I sit up like electric shocked. I start ripping the pictures of Angel Juan off my walls. Tomorrow.

"Go away now!" I growl, shredding the picture of us in the desert, shredding Angel Juan. Shredding myself.

After all the pictures are gone I slam my arms against the wall of the shed again, again, and crumple

9

down into a shred-bed of eyes and mouths and bass guitars and cactus needles. I am not going to let myself cry.

When I wake up I reach for him—his hair crisp against my lips, his hot-water-bottle heat. I crawl clawing and sliding over the torn photographs to the door. Out in the empty garden it is already tomorrow.

I don't go to school. I lie in the bed of ruined pictures for hours. The shed is dark. Smells of soil and sawdust. Blue and yellow sunflower bruises bloom on my arms.

I remember the time when I was a kid and I first met the little black-haired boy named Angel Juan. He was the first person that made me feel I belonged—like I wasn't just some freaky pain-gobbling goblin nobody understood. Then he had to go back to Mexico with his parents, Marquez and Gabriela Perez, and his brothers and sisters, Angel Miguel, Angel Pedro, Angelina and Serafina. I didn't see him for years. But it was okay. I had myself. I knew that I could feel things. Not just smashing anger and loneliness. But love too. It was inside of me. And then on my birth-day a few years later Angel Juan came back.

Now it's different because he doesn't *have* to go away. He wants to. And also we've done it—the wild love thing. So I feel like I need him to put me back together every night. After his kisses and hugs it feels like without them my body will fall apart into pieces.

I get up and take the shoe boxes out from under the bed. They are filled with newspaper clippings I used to have on my walls—before Angel Juan. "Whales Die in Toxic Waters." "Beautiful Basketball God Gets Disease." "Family Burned in Gas Explosion." "Murderer Collects Victims' Body Parts." Even after Angel Juan I cut them out when we had a fight or something but I'd always hide them under my bed. Pictures of all the pain I could find. A pain game.

"What a world!" says the Wicked Witch in *The Wizard of Oz* before she melts.

The only way I used to be able to stand being in this world was to hold it in my hands, in front of my eyes. That way I thought—it can't get me or some-thing. But when I had Angel Juan I only wanted to touch and see *him*. He was the only way I've ever really been able to escape.

Now it's the pain game again.

Night.

Across the garden my family is together eating vegetarian lasagna, edible flower salad and fruit-juice-sweetened apple pie. They are laughing in the beeswax candlelight, talking about the next movie they are going to make and looking out over the ruins of the magician's castle through stained-glass flowers. I wonder if they wonder where I am. They probably think I'm having a picnic at the beach in the back of Angel Juan's red pickup truck. Or maybe by now they all know that Angel Juan is gone. Maybe he told them before me.

There is a knock on my door.

It's him. He's back. I made this whole thing up. He is here with his pickup truck full of blankets and Fig Newtons for a moonlight picnic.

But then I hear my almost-mom Weetzie Bat's voice.

"Honey-honey," she says. "Aren't you going to eat tonight?"

I don't move. It's like I'm a statue of me.

Weetzie opens the door slow. I didn't lock it this

morning. Should have. She's carrying the lamp shaped like a globe that I gave to my dad a long time ago. She plugs it in and the world lights up.

Weetzie looks around at the torn-up pictures of Angel Juan and the scattered newspaper clippings. Then she sits down next to me on the floor. The blue oceans make her shine.

Suddenly remember. Lifted into the light. Somebody playing piano. Vanilla-gardenia. Weetzie's white-gold halo hair. It's the day I was left in a basket on the doorstep and Weetzie found me like those changeling things in stories, the ones that fairies leave in baskets, strange kids with some mark on them or the wrong color eyes. My eyes are purple. In a way I want Weetzie to lift me up into the light again. But more I want to sink back into the darkness where I came from. I want to drown under the newspaper pain and the shreds of Angel Juan.

"Go away," I growl at Weetzie. But she knows me too well by now. And I feel too old and weak to bite and scratch the way I did when I was a little kid before Angel Juan came. So she just sits there with me not touching, not talking for a long time. I wonder if she can see the bruises on my arms.

Finally she says, "I wanted to bring you something magic that would make everything okay." She must have already heard about Angel Juan. "But now I know that magic's not that simple. I wish I could give you a lamp with a genie in it to make all your wishes come true. But you're a genie. Your own genie. Just believe in that."

Supposedly a long time ago Weetzie wished on her genie lamp and that's how she met my dad and how her best friend Dirk McDonald met his true love Duck Drake and how they all ended up living together. Weetzie thinks life's so slinkster-cool as she would say because all her wishes came true.

But right now I don't believe in that magic crap. I don't believe in anything. All I want is to find Angel Juan.

"I want to go to New York," I say. My voice sounds gritty. My throat hurts like my voice is made of broken glass.

"To find him or to find you?" Weetzie asks.

Why is she asking me stuff like this like she thinks she knows so much? I want her to leave me alone.

I look at the globe lamp. If somebody said to me,

You can go all over the world by yourself looking at everything—all the death and all the love—or you can sleep inside the globe lamp with the echo of the oceans as your lullaby and the continents floating around you like blankets with Angel Juan beside you, I would choose to sleep with Angel Juan in a place he can never leave.

To find him.

Niña Bruja,

The building on the front of this card looks like a firefly tree at night.

The acoustics in the subways are good for playing music. I close my eyes underground to try to see you jammin' on your drums, your hair all flying out like wild petals, beat pulsing in your flower-stem neck.

I have breakfast in Harlem. You would love the grits. You eat like a kitten dipping your chin.

I built a tree house in the park. I think the trees have spirits living in them but the one in this tree doesn't seem to mind me being here.

Being in the trees helps me see outside of myself. So does riding the Ferris wheel at Coney Island. Coney Island is closed in the winter but I met a man who knows how to get in.

I saw a saint parade with all these little girls wearing wings. Remember the wings you used to wear? I thought the little girls were all going to float off their floats into the sky. Afterwards one came over to me and handed me this little silver medal with St. Raphael on it. He is a wound healer. He is riding on a fish. I hope he watches over you.

In Mexico people wear hummingbird amulets around their necks to show they are searching for love. Here people pretend that they aren't. Searching.

I hope that you are being sweet to yourself. I wish that I could comb the snarl-balls out of your hair and hear you purr.

I don't have an address yet but I'll write to you again soon.

I love you.

Angel Juan

Dear Angel Juan,

You used to guard my sleep like a panther biting back my pain with the edge of your teeth. You carried me into the dark dream jungle, loping past the hungry vines, crossing the shiny fish-scale river. We left my tears behind in a chiming silver pool. We left my sorrow in the muddy hollows. When I woke up you were next to me, damp and matted, your eyes hazy, trying to remember the way I clung to you, how far down we went.

Was the journey too far, Angel Juan? Did we go too far?

School's out pretty soon. Can't wait. I hardly talk to anybody there. Sometimes I feel like I come from another planet. Planet of the Witch Babies where the sky is purple, the stars are cameras, the flowers are drums and all the boys look like Angel Juan. When I'm at school I wish I came from my own planet. And I want to go back.

I've got some money from *The Goat Guys*, the movie my dad directed about the slam-jam band my

17

almost-sister Cherokee and her soul-love Raphael and me and Angel Juan are in. Were in—before. In the movie we all played us.

The angel medallion that came in the mail sleeps in the hollow part of my neck. I can't send a letter telling that or anything else to Angel Juan.

I don't know where he is. But I'm going to look for him.

The only thing is where to stay in New York. So I ask Weetzie about Charlie Bat's place.

Weetzie's dad Charlie Bat died a long time ago before I was born. But Weetzie begged her mom Brandy-Lynn not to let go of his old apartment in the Village. It's like she doesn't want to admit that he's dead.

Weetzie is sitting in the room with the dried roses and painted fans all over the walls and the stained-glass pyramid-palm-tree windows that look out on the canyon. From here you can see a few blue pools like the canyon's eyes and the waves of palm, euca-lyptus and oleander like the canyon's swirly green hair. The canyon talks in different voices. In the day she growls with traffic, but real early or late at night she sings with mockingbirds and you can hear her wind-chime jewelry. Angel Juan and I used to sneak over garden walls and swim in the pool eyes at night. We used to climb the trees, tangling in the braids of leaves, and Angel Juan told me he was going to build us a tree house someday. His dad Marquez, who makes frames and furniture, taught him how to build tree houses.

In our house that feels like a tree house some-times—deep in the canyon, nested in leaves—Weetzie's working on the script for the next movie she and my dad are making. It's a ghost story.

"I'm going to New York," I say. "Could I stay at Charlie Bat's?"

"Are you sure you want to go to New York, honey?"

"I'm going to New York," I say. I start to nibble at my fingernails, chew my cuticles.

Weetzie goes over to her 1920's dressing table with the round mirror and the lotus-blossom lights. The little genie lamp is sitting there—still gold but empty of genies and wishes now. Weetzie takes an old photo album out of a dressing table drawer. It's so old that almost all the pile of the pink velvet has worn down around the gold curlicues and cupids. It's so old that it was probably red velvet once, a long time ago. Weetzie sits on her seashell-shaped love seat that is the same velvet pink as the photo album and pats it for me to sit next to her. I climb up the side and perch, looking over her shoulder instead. Inside the photo album is a picture of a tall skinny man with sunken eyes and bones like the guys in those old black-and-white silent movies. Kind of like Valentino but a lot thinner and not so healthy-looking. The man has his arm around a little blonde woman with a big lipsticky smile and slidey gold mules on her feet. They seem really in love standing in front of this cherry yellow T-bird clinking champagne glasses: Weetzie's mom and dad when they were young. Before Brandy-Lynn and Charlie and the champagne glasses and the T-bird got smashed. Before Brandy-Lynn kicked Charlie out and he went to New York and died there.

Weetzie shows me a picture of her and her real

daughter, my almost-sister Cherokee, with Charlie from the time when they went to visit him just before he died. It was taken in one of those photo booths. Cherokee was just a baby then with little tufts of white hair like a Kewpie doll or something. Weetzie looks exactly the same as she does now—elf mom— maybe a little skinnier and her hair was a little shorter, kind of spiky. But Charlie doesn't look much like a silent-movie star anymore. He looks more like a ghost. There's a spooky light around his head and his eyeballs are rolled up. Weetzie has her arm around him really tight and her fingers pressed into his shoulder.

She's never held on to me like that.

Not that I'd let her.

"I think people leave here before we think they're gone," Weetzie whispers as she looks at the picture. "And when you're with them you know it. Part of you knows it—that they've left. But you don't let yourself really accept it. And then later you think about it and you know you knew."

I can see her going back to that time, trying to find her dad.

beautiful boys

"We had to walk up eight flights of stairs to his apartment in the dark and every time he whistled 'Rag Mop' to us—you know, 'R-A-G-G M-O-P-P Rag Mop doodely-doo' to make us laugh. But that time he was quiet. When we got to the apartment he went and stood by the window and shut his eyes, listening to the echoes of kids playing outside way down there in the distance, and he said, 'It sounds like when I was a little boy in Brooklyn and we ran around the streets in the twilight, hoping it would never get all the way dark so we'd have to go in. Kids playing sound the same wherever you are. They sound so happy. They don't know what's in store for them.'

"I said it could still be happy, like kids playing in the street before they have to go in for dinner. My friends and I, we live like that. Come live with us. But he was far away already." Weetzie closes her eyes. It's real quiet for a minute and I can hear the canyon tossing her hair and her wind-chime earrings clinking like Charlie and Brandy-Lynn's champagne glasses in the photograph.

I wonder what it would be like to talk to Charlie

Bat. I bet he would get it. He died from drugs all alone. He was an artist but he didn't make pretty things. Weetzie says he wrote movies and plays about monsters, but they were really about the monster feelings inside.

"I miss him so much. But I can't even dream about him," Weetzie says.

What she says reminds me of Angel Juan. Sometimes it almost feels like Angel Juan is dead too.

It's like Weetzie's reading my mind for a second. "You really need to look for him, don't you?"

I am busy with my cuticle gnaw. "Can I go see Charlie Bat?" I mumble.

Weetzie stares at me like she's seen a ghost. "Lanky lizards," she whispers.

"I mean Charlie *Bat's*—his place," I say.

Weetzie nods, looking at her photo album.

In a way I'm glad she's into letting me go. But another part of me wishes she didn't want me to. It seems like she's thinking more about Charlie Bat than about me.

Dear Angel Juan,

Why haven't you written again? It's been three weeks one day and three hours since the last time I saw you in the fog.

I try to dream about you but I can't. The harder I try to find you, the farther away you get. Instead I dream about my real mother Vixanne Wigg.

There's a knock on the shed door and I think— Angel Juan—and open it. But it's a tall lanky lanka in a blonde wig. She has purple crazy eyes. And they are the same as mine. She's my mother. I try to close the door but she shoves herself inside. Her wig falls off. Long black hair pours down wrapping me up like vine arms. She forces apples down my throat and needles into my fingers.

I wake up choked, prickly. It's one thing to read fairy tales when you are a regular kid but what about when your mother is a real witch? Or maybe it's the same for all kids these days. People really do inject apples with needles full of poison and hand them out at doorways. The good thing about fairy tales, though, is that there is always a fairy godmother and/or a prince to take the curse away.

Sometimes when this same dream used to wake me up in the middle of the night, you said, "The curse is broken," and put me back to sleep with lullaby kisses.

Maybe Vixanne can help me find you.

I get up, put on my cowboy-boot roller skates and go out into a fog as green as the fog was green on the night before Angel Juan left.

I haven't been to the big pink house in the hills for years but somehow I know exactly how to get back there. The way our dog Tiki-Tee keeps going back to where he was born, the place my family uses as a studio now. He slinks out and trots through the canyon down the street named for the newest moon all the way to the cottage. Whenever he's missing, we know we'll find him there curled up in between the stone gnomes under the rosebushes.

Just like Tiki-Tee finds the cottage, I find the place where I was born. It blooms out of the fog. It's all falling apart now. The driveway is empty and the windows are caked with dust. Maybe Vixanne moved away.

I take off my skates, creep up to the door and knock. No one answers. The door swings open by itself and I slip in, skidding on my socks.

There's the hallway lined with mirrors where I freaked myself once. Now I know they're me but I want to smash my reflections. So in the mirror I'll look like I feel. Pieces. But if you break a mirror there are just more whole little yous in every piece.

I go into the dusty sunken room. Empty. Cold air burns in the empty fireplace. There are squished tubes of paint and canvases everywhere. And lots of big portraits of Vixanne Wigg in colors like tropical flowers—almost glow-in-the-dark.

Vixanne powdery-pink and sparkle-platinum as Jayne Mansfield chomp-gnawing off a cluster chunk of crystally-white dry-ice rock candy. Vixanne lounging in a fluorescent green jungle tied up in her own jungle-green writhe-vine hair. Dressed in milky apple blossoms and holding a grimacy shrively monkey-face apple. Wreath of giant blue and orange butterflies around her head. With a rainbow-jewel-scaled mermaid tail. A ripple-haunched horse from the waist down. Vixanne with black roses tattooed on her naked chest. All of the Vixannes staring at me with purple eyes.

I go up to the one with the tattoo. Pain-ink flowers. Meat-eating roses in a demony garden. The paint is rich and smooth like batter. I wish Vixanne would paint me:

Angel Juan's name tattooed on my heart in a wreath of black roses.

Something rustles. Heavy crunched silk. I turn around.

"You've been gone a long time," says a voice. She sounds tired.

Vixanne's long dark hair that she used to wear under the Jayne Mansfield wig is hacked short and kind of uneven like she did it herself. It reminds me of me when Cherokee cut off my hair with toenail scissors when we were babies. Vixanne wears a black silk dress with watery patterns in it. She is so different from the glam lanka I remember.

"Remember those photographs you gave me?" she says.

When I found her the first time, I gave her some pictures I took. An old woman shaking her fist and screaming at the sun. A man who was too young to be dying. Me looking like a little lost loon waif thing. I wanted my mother to have something when I left. I wanted her to see.

"At first I put them away and didn't look at them but I kept thinking about you. You were so little skating around with that camera seeing all the pain."

Her eyes roll in her head. I want to leave but instead I sit down and start playing with the paints on the table. It feels good to squeeze the tubes of paint. Smell the stinkster turpentine. Vixanne sits down next to me. I want to paint a picture of Angel Juan. As big as life. A boy that will never leave.

"I like to be alone," Vixanne says. "I've started painting. I'm not anyone's slave now."

I listen to the sound of her voice and feel all the twilight purple eyes watching me while my hand moves by itself in the shadowy room.

Maybe hours go by.

"I look things right in the eye now. That's the best way. Right in the eye and without anything to make it easier," says Vixanne.

I look down and drop my paintbrush. It skids

across the floor. Instead of Angel Juan I've made a picture of a man with big teeth eating a cake that drips icing all over his face and hands. It gives me a creepy-crawly-heebee-jeebee feeling.

I pretend the goose bumps studding my arms are 'cause I'm cold.

I take black paint and wipe out the man with the cake like he was never there. "I don't want to look at anything or anybody except for Angel Juan."

Vixanne shakes her head. Then she says, "You have to leave now, Witch Baby. You can come back after your journey."

She goes to the door with me and I put on my skates. I wonder how I will ever make it home and then all the way to New York. The parts of my body feel held together by strings you could cut with a scissors.

"Remember to look in the eye. That's what you taught me," Vixanne says. "Look at your own darkness."

I leave my mother all complete in a gnarly snarly forest of herself, and the puppet parts of my body skate away into the fog.

I am going to leave.

I think that Weetzie misses her dead dad more than she will miss me.

Vixanne is busy painting pictures of her own face.

The rest of my family is working on their movie. It's about ghosts but if anybody knows about being haunted it's me.

In the shed by the light of the globe lamp I pack up my bat-shaped backpack. Angel Juan has taken my mind and my heart away and his ghost is trapped in the empty places that are left. Not so I feel like he's with me. Just like always remembering that he's not. So it's not like I can just sit around here waiting. I have to go find him.

I am going to take a cab to the airport because everybody's too busy to drive me. My dad is in the desert by himself meditating about the new movie. Weetzie has a yoga class that she hates to miss.

Just before I leave I go into the kitchen. Blue and yellow handpainted sunflower tiles. Stained-glass sunflower skylight. Reminds me of the bruises

I gave myself when Angel Juan left.

Weetzie puts out a glass of honey lemonade and a stack of pumpkin pancakes for me but I can't eat anything.

"New York makes my nerves feel like this," she says, sliding something down the butcher-block table to me. "Maybe if you wear it yours won't."

It's a skeleton charm bracelet. I pick it up and the skeletons click their plastic bones. Weetzie usually gives people stuff with cherubs, flowers and stars. I guess witch babies get bone things.

"I'm sorry I can't take you to the airport," she says. "Are you sure you'll be all right?"

I roll my eyes and don't talk. I'm afraid I'll start to cry like some watery-knee weaselette.

"Well, remember, Mr. Mallard and Mr. Meadows will give you the key to the apartment and they'll help you if you need anything."

The cab is honking outside. Weetzie tries to kiss me but I am out the door already. Maybe she should have been a little more clutch like in that picture of her and her dad Charlie Bat where she looks like she'll never let go.

Dear Angel Juan,

    I'm on a plane. I imagine you out there on a cloud, playing your bass and grinning at me, wearing chunky black shoes and Levi's with rips at the knees. I imagine the rest of the band and it is one heavenly combo—Jimi and Jim and John and Bob and Elvis— all the dudes you are into.

    All those guys are dead.

    So I think about you down on the ground with me.

    We are at the movies. The air-conditioned air on our bare arms and the crackle and smell of the popcorn and the crackle of the film in between the previews that is the same sound as the popcorn almost. And we're holding hands and we know we'll hold hands on the way to the truck and even while we're driving home in between clutch shifting and then we'll get into bed together and hold each other in our sleep and wake up together in the morning and slurp fruit shakes and munch jammy peanut-butter-banana sandwiches.

    It's summer. We're on the wooden deck. We've been in the sun all day and just had a hot tub. You're play-ing bass and I'm playing my drums. Our music weaves together like our bodies in the night. The lanterns are lit and the air smells like honeysuckle, barbecue smoke and incense. The dark canyon is rustling with heat around us.

We're in Joshua Tree. We sit on a huge flat rock still warm from the day and you comb the tangles out of my hair and it doesn't even hurt. We eat honey-nut Guru Chews and watch the full moon rise. The moon makes my insides stir. Then we hear something. You stop combing my tangles. Music. Pouring from somewhere in the empty desert. It's like fountains in the sand or sky islands. "Celestial music," you say. No one else hears it.

I tell myself I have to stop thinking words like celestial and heavenly. And angel. But that last one is hard.

I load the cab with the globe lamp, my camera, my roller skates and my bat-shaped backpack. The angel medallion is around my neck. As the cab drives along the highway from the airport into Manhattan I shake my wrist so that the skeletons on my charm bracelet do their bone jig. Looking up at all the big buildings and seeing the crowd scurrying along, I know what Weetzie meant about her nerves and the skeletons. New York is not a Weetzie-city. Weetzie is a kid of the city where movies are made and it's always sunny, where Marilyn's ghost rises up out of her spiky birdy footprints to dance on beams of light with red lacquer dragons in front of the Chinese Theater, and James Dean's head star-watches with you at the observatory like a fallen star somebody found and put on a pedestal; a city where you can only tell the seasons by the peonies or pumpkins or poinsettias at the florists'.

But me, maybe I fit in a place like this. Maybe the cold inside of me will seem less cold in this winter. Maybe the tall buildings will make the brick walls I build for myself seem smaller. Maybe the noises in my head will quiet down in the middle of all the other noises. Or maybe my cold and walls and noise will get worse.

It looks frosty out and the store windows are filled with red velvet bows, white fur, plastic reindeer with long eyelashes and flaming Christmas trees and for the first time I realize that I won't be with my almost-family for the holidays. I was so busy thinking about finding Angel Juan that I didn't even realize that before.

"Where are you from?" the driver asks after a while. He has a beautiful island voice and it makes me feel warmer just hearing it. For a second I think about Angel Juan and me sharing a ginger beer on the rocks behind a fall of see-through water and ruby-red flowers that he keeps catching and sticking in my tangles.

Another cab swerves into our lane and my driver slams the brakes. I'm jolted out of Jamaica.

"Los Angeles."

"Oh, Angel City. You won't be finding too many of those here. Especially in the meat district."

I look out the window at the meat-packing plants lining the cobblestone streets by the river. Men are unloading marbly sides of beef from a truck. There isn't much sign of Christmas out here.

"Of what?" I ask.

"Angels," he says.

"I just need to find one," I say.

We pull up to the brownstone building where Charlie Bat lived and died. The driver says, "Well, if you're looking for angels in New York, at least this is a good place."

"What?"

"I've heard things about that building, that's all," he says, helping me unload. "Magic stuff. Good luck."

I zip up my leather jacket and hand him his money. "Thanks," I say, thinking he is just trying to be nice about the angel thing. But when I see how he is staring up at the brownstone I wonder what he meant. He has this look on his face—kind of wonder or something. Charlie's building doesn't look magic to me though. Just old and ready to crumble. A few of the windows are cracked. It reminds me of an old vaudeville guy who wears baggy dirty suits and can't dance anymore, and somebody beat him up and smashed his glasses.

I stand on the curb and watch the cab drive away. It's dark now. When did that happen? No time for sunset here. Just a fast change of backdrop like in a store window display.

Some dancer girls colt by. They look like their

feet hurt but they don't care because they've been dancing. A woman holds on to her kid in a different way from how parents hold kids where I come from. She is gripping the little mittened hand and the kid's face looks pale and almost old. Two men in tweed coats and mufflers go into the building. One walks with a cane and wears sunglasses even though it's night and the other is carrying a bag of groceries. I can see French bread and flowers sticking out of the top. The flowers look like they are wondering what they are doing in this city like they flew here by mistake and saw these two men and decided that their bag was probably the best place to land.

I want to take photographs for the first time since Angel Juan left. But I don't. I won't use my eyes for anything except finding Angel Juan.

I try to picture Weetzie coming here, a long time ago with Cherokee tucked in her arms, all excited to show her new baby to her dad. She must have felt kind of weird though, standing in front of this building in the middle of the meat-packing district. Maybe that's when she decided to stop eating meat when she saw the dead cows unloaded from the trucks. She must have been freaked about Charlie living here all alone. I wish I got to come meet Charlie too. I wonder if he would have thought I was his real granddaughter like Cherokee.

Inside the lobby is dark and musty-dusty. There is an elevator but it has an "Out of Order" sign on it so I find the stairs.

The stairs are even darker. As I walk up I think I hear somebody whistling a tune. What is it? Sort of silly but also sad, like whoever is whistling wants to stop but can't or like a circus clown with a smile painted on.

I stop on the third floor and knock. A gray-haired slinkster man answers. He is one of the men in the tweed coats I saw on the street.

"I'm Witch Baby."

"Witch Baby! Come in. Weetzie has been calling all day to see if you've arrived. Come in."

The little warm apartment is covered—floor, walls, ceiling—in faded Persian pomegranate-courtyard-garden carpets. There are lots of velvety loungy couches and chairs that make me feel like curling up like Tiki-Tee does in the bend of my knees, lots of overstuffed tapestry pillows and bookshelves stuffed with old leather books. See-through veils hanging from the ceiling. Tall viny iron candlesticks blooming big candles frosted with dripped wax. What it makes me think about mostly is crawling inside that genie lamp Weetzie has at home—what it would be like in there.

The man who walked with a cane is arranging the flowers in a golden vase that almost looks like the genie lamp.

"Meadows, Charlie Bat's grandchild has arrived," says the first man. The man named Meadows comes over and holds out his hand. He has a sweet boy-face even though he is probably almost as old as the other man and he is still wearing his dark glasses.

"That's Meadows and I'm Mallard," the first man says. "For some reason your mother thought that my name was funny. Something to do with ducks. I didn't get it."

In my family duck means a pounceable guy who likes guys, which is what Mallard is—a very grown-up gray duck—but I don't know how to explain it. "In my family names are a kind of weird thing," I say.

"I can tell," says Mallard. "Now where did they

come up with Witch Baby? You are much too pretty for that. She looks like a skinny, boyish, young Sophia Loren hiding under a head full of tangles." He turns to Meadows, who smiles and nods.

I sure don't think I look like any gorgeous Italian actress with a big chest. "Weetzie tried to name me Lily but it never stuck," I say.

"Lily sounds right for you," says Meadows. "May we call you Lily?"

"Sure."

Mallard says, "You must be exhausted, Lily. Would you like to sleep on our couch? It might be more comfortable than your grandfather's apartment. There isn't any furniture there."

"He wasn't really my true grandfather," I say. "He was my almost-grandfather. He's Weetzie's dad and she met my dad when she was working at Duke's because she had wished for him on the genie lamp that Dirk—that's her best friend—Dirk's grandma Fifi gave her and she also wished for a duck for Dirk and a house for them to live in and Fifi died and Dirk met Duck and Weetzie and My Secret Agent Lover Man—that's my dad's name—all moved into Fifi's

cottage but then Weetzie wanted a baby and my dad
didn't want one so she had Cherokee with Dirk and
Duck and my dad left and met Vixanne Wigg who is
a lanka witch and stayed with her but then he came
back to Weetzie and one day Vixanne brought me and
left me on the doorstep in a basket and Weetzie and
my dad and Dirk and Duck made me like part of the
family but in a way I'm not."

"Very confusing," says Mallard. "Sometime you
must draw us a family tree."

"Okay. But I'll be okay at Charlie's."

"What have you brought with you?" Mallard is
looking at the globe lamp.

"Weetzie thinks it'll be good luck."

Meadows nods all solemn. "Apotropaic."

"What?"

"It means something to ward off evil. You will be
comfortable wherever you sleep. Can you have dinner
with us tomorrow night?"

"Sure."

Mallard hands me a set of keys on a big silver
ring. My wrist is so skinny it could almost be a
bracelet.

"We know a macrobiotic place with the best tofu pie," Meadows says.

Soybean-curd pie doesn't sound so great to me but I don't say anything.

"Meanwhile, you must take some of our groceries." Mallard goes to the kitchen and comes back with a paper bag full of food.

"That's okay."

"You must. You have to eat and it's not a great idea to be running around alone at night. I'll show you up to Charlie's place."

I say good-bye to Meadows and walk up six flights of stairs with Mallard, the keys, the food and a stack of blankets to Charlie Bat's apartment.

Mallard opens the door and lets me in. "No one's lived here for a long time," he says. "We take care of it and we tried to make it as nice as possible for you but still . . ."

The apartment is smaller than the one downstairs and it's cold and empty except for an old trunk thing made out of leather. The paint on the walls is peeling. But there is a view of the city, not a speck of dust-grunge anywhere and a Persian rug like the ones downstairs on the floor. Suddenly I feel so tired I want to fall into the garden of the rug, just keep falling forever through pink leaves.

"Now you'd better eat something and get right to bed," Mallard says, putting down the blankets. "We thought you'd be safe and comfortable on the rug. There's no phone but you just run downstairs anytime if you need anything."

He hands me the groceries. "Remember dinner tomorrow. Good night."

As he closes the door I feel loneliness tunnel through my body. I look inside the bag of food and there's granola, milk, strawberries, bananas, peanut butter, bagels, mineral water and peppermint tea. I sit on the old trunk and eat a banana-and-peanut-butter bagel sandwich to try to fill up the tunnel the loneliness made. Then I try to open the trunk but it's locked. I go stand by the window.

New York is like a forbidden box. I am looking down into it. There's the firefly building on Angel Juan's card and the dark danger streets. All these sparkling electric treasures and all these strange scary things that shouldn't have been let out but they all were. And somewhere, down there, with the angels and the demons, is Angel Juan.

I plug in the globe lamp and lie down on Mallard and Meadows's carpet under the blankets in a corner.

"Apotropaic," Meadows said.

I hold on to the globe like it is my heart I am trying to hold together. But my heart isn't solid and full of light like the lamp. It's cracked and empty and I just lie there not trying to hold it together anymore, letting my dry no-tear sobs break it up into little pieces, wanting to dream about Angel Juan—at least that.

But when I do fall asleep it's like being buried with nothing except dirt filling up my eyes.

Morning. Strawberry sky dusted with white winter powder-sugar sun. And nobody to munch on it with.

I drink some tea, get my camera and go out into the bright cold.

As soon as I start skating I get the sick empty feeling in my stomach again. But it's worse this time. How am I ever supposed to find Angel Juan in this city? It is the clutchiest thing I have ever tried to do.

What made me think I could find him? Here is this whole city full of monuments and garbage and Chinese food and cannolis and steaks and drug dealers and paintings and subways and cigarettes and mannequins and a million other things and I am looking for one kind-of-small boy who left me. As if I know where he would be. As if he wanted me to find him. Why am I here at all?

I see men crumple-slumped in the gutters like empty coats and women who hide their bodies and look like their heads hurt. I see couples of men that look older and thinner than they should and kids that look harder than everybody pretends kids look. Everything vicious and broken and my eyes ache dry and tearless in my sockets. I can't even take pictures.

Subway.

In Angel Juan's letter: *I close my eyes underground to try to see you jammin' on your drums, your hair all flying out like petals, beat pulsing in your flower-stem neck.*

I go down, tilting my roller-skate wheels into the steps and holding on to the rail so I don't free-fall.

The trains are all I can hear burning through the emptiness inside of me like acid on a cut—no music. There aren't any boys playing guitars down here, their eyelashes grazing their cheekbones to protect them from the fluorescent light, their bodies shivery like guitar strings.

I get on a train and stand in between all the padded people with puffy faces and blind eyes.

I climb up the subway stairs with my skates still on, using my arms to hoist me.

On the street I see a scary-looking girl with jungle-wild hair and eyes and then I see it's me reflected in a stained oval mirror that's propped against some trash cans. I drag the mirror back to the apartment holding it away from me so I don't have to see my face.

I'm thrashed and mashed—starving and ready to cry again. My arms and legs are shaking and I can hardly make it up to the ninth floor carrying the mirror, even with my skates off. My head is full of wound-pictures, my camera is empty and I feel farther away from Angel Juan than ever.

On the door of Charlie Bat's apartment is a note.

Lily: Meet us in the lobby for dinner at 6:00. Your benevolent almost-almost uncles, Meadows and Mallard.

I would rather collapse in the pomegranate garden of the Persian carpet and go to sleep forever, but I make myself wash my face and go downstairs.

Mallard and Meadows are waiting for me in the lobby wearing their tweed coats.

"How was your day?" Mallard asks.

I shrug.

"You look tired. Did you eat anything?"

"We are going to buy you a nice big dinner," Meadows says.

They walk on either side of me like tweedy angels or like halves of a pair of wings as we go through the streets past the meat-packing plants. Meadows's cane taps on the cobblestones. Some six-foot-tall skulkster drag queens wait in the shadows flashing at the passing cars. Mallard picks a wildflower that grows up between the stones. It's a strange-looking lily and I wonder why it's growing here in the middle of the meat and dark.

The restaurant is hidden on a narrow winding side street. We come in out of the cold.

This place is like somebody's enchanted living room. There's flowered paper on the walls. If you look close you can see tiny mysterious creatures peering out from between the wallpaper flowers and the lavender-and-white frosted rosette-shaped glass lights strung around the ceiling blink on and off, making it look like the creatures are dancing. On every table there are burning towers of wax roses that give off a honey smell. The music isn't like anything I ever heard before. It's crickety and rivery. The waitress has a dreamy-face, long blonde curls and a tiny waist. She is wearing a crochet lace dress. She serves us tea that smells like a forest and makes my headache go away. Then she brings huge mismatched antique floral china plates heaped with brown rice and these vegetables that I've never seen before but taste like what goddesses would eat if they ate their vegetables. Miso-oniony, golden-pumpkiny, sweety-lotusy, sesame-seaweedy. The food makes me stop shaking.

"How did you find this place?" I ask.

"We try everything but this is the best," says Meadows.

"This food helps us write better," says Mallard. "We commune better when we aren't digesting animals."

"What do you write?" I ask.

Mallard looks at Meadows. Then he says, "We write about . . . phenomena. Supernatural phenomena."

"Ghosts," says Meadows.

"Like what my family's movie is about."

"Really?" says Mallard. "That must be why they sent you here."

"I don't think so."

"Maybe they thought you'd find a ghost here." Mallard chuckles.

"But you won't," Meadows says. "We haven't found a single ghost in our building."

The waitress brings more tea and a cart of desserts that she says are made without any sugar or milk stuff. Mallard and Meadows and I share a piece of creamy you-wouldn't-believe-it's-soy-curd tofu pie, a piece of scrumptious yam pie and a dense kiss piece of caroby almond cake. The carob reminds me of the walk Angel Juan and I took before he left when we stepped on the St. John's bread pods and they cracked open and smelled like chocolate.

Why aren't you here? I think. Why aren't you here, Angel Juan?

We're sitting on cushions in Mallard and Meadows's apartment listening to Indian sitar music. If I close my eyes I can see a goddess with lots of arms and almondy eyes moving her head from side to side like it's not part of her neck, hypnotizing a garden of snakes. Maybe she's hiding behind the veils that hang from the ceiling.

"Feel better?" Meadows asks.

"Yes, thanks for dinner. I'll take you guys out tomorrow night."

"We have to go on a trip, Lily," Mallard says. "We leave tonight."

"It's for our book," says Meadows. He turns his head to me. He isn't wearing his glasses and suddenly his eyes catch the light. I have this feeling that he can see. "We are visiting a house in Ireland where a woman's father keeps appearing."

"Except he's dead," says Mallard.

"Except he's about this big," says Meadows, holding his hands a few inches apart. "Sitting on her teacup."

"If you want you can stay at our place instead of upstairs while we're away," says Mallard. "It might be more comfortable."

He looks very serious and I wonder if he's thinking about how Charlie Bat died up there. I hadn't even thought about it last night because I'd been so tired and crazed about Angel Juan: Charlie Bat probably OD'd in the same corner where I slept. But I kind of like being in my almost-grandpa's place.

I try not to show how I feel about my new friends going away, how I know tonight with its macro-heaven dinner and goddess music will fade, leaving me just as empty as before, loneliness attacking all my cells like a disease.

"Thanks but I'll be okay," I say.

"Did you sleep all right last night?" Meadows asks.

"I didn't even dream."

"We'll leave keys to our place," says Mallard. "In

case you change your mind. Use the phone anytime and whatever is in the fridge." Then he goes, "I'm sorry we won't be with you for Christmas."

"But we'll be back New Year's Eve day," says Meadows.

When I leave he hands me the meaty white lily Mallard picked.

I carry the lily in front of me up the dark staircase like it is a lantern. And then a creepster thing happens. Light *does* start coming out of the flower. At first I think from the flower but then the light starts jumping all over the walls in front of me lighting the way. Someone is whistling somewhere. No, the *light* is whistling.

I get to the top of the stairs on the ninth floor. The light goes out and the whistling stops. I must have imagined it because I'm tired. Maybe I'm going crazy.

I think that all of me is broken. Not just my heart which cracked the night Angel Juan told me he was going away. Not just my body slammed with the sadness I see with no one there to put me back together in bed at night. Now it feels like my mind too.

In Charlie's apartment I put the flower in a teacup and look at myself in the mirror I found on the street. I can hardly stand to see my face. Pinchy and hungry-looking. I don't need a hummingbird around my neck for people to see I am searching for love.

I wrap the mirror in a sheet and hit it with a hammer I found in a kitchen drawer. Feeling the smooth whole thing turn into sharp jags shifting under the sheet, spilling out all bright and broken. I don't even care about seven years' bad luck.

But then I look into the jags and there I am—still all one scary-looking Witch Baby in every piece.

I just want to disappear. Everything to stop.

That's when the whistling flower lights up again. I sit staring as the light jumps out of the flower, all around the apartment and lands inside the globe lamp, making it day all over the world. And instead of whistling the light starts singing a song—soft and snap-crackly like an old reel of film.

"R-A-G-G M-O-P-P, Rag Mop doodely-doo."

Lanky lizards, as Weetzie would say. Maybe I am cracking up.

"Who are you?"

The voice doesn't answer. Only keeps on singing—"R-A-G-G M-O-P-P."

Why would somebody write a whole song about a mop made out of rags? And why would they spell it?

The light dances out of the globe lamp and all over the walls to the tune it is whistling. It's jiggling doing a jig.

Then it flashes in a piece of broken mirror and I go over to look but instead of me I see this guy.

He's black and white and flickery like an old movie; he's wearing a rumpled black suit and a top hat like a spooky circus ringmaster. Light is filling him up like he swallowed it and it is coming through his pores, making him kind of fidget-dance around in the mirror like one of the plastic skeletons on my charm bracelet. His eyes are ringed with dark shadows like the negatives of two moons before a rain. He wrinkles his forehead, moves his hands and opens and closes his mouth.

"Who are you?" I ask.

Finally he coughs, clears his throat and says, "You're my baby's witch baby and you are witnessing a spectacular spectral spectacle sort of."

I try to look deeper in the mirror but it's like a smog-mirage in L.A. when the heat ripples and blurs like water or like looking into the Pacific Ocean so dull with crud it's like a smoggy sky. I can't see too well but I know it's him.

Charlie B., Chucky Bat, C. Bat, Mr C. Bbbbb-b-Bat. My almost-grandpa-Bat Charles.

He's a lot like he was in the pictures Weetzie showed me but if he didn't look healthy then he really doesn't look so well now and he's not in color anymore.

What do you say to a ghost? "I'm not Weetzie's real kid."

"You look real to me."

"I don't feel like it lately."

"Neither do I." He laughs soft. I think about the pop in the film before a Charlie Chaplin movie starts. "We have some things in common."

"Yeah. I mean besides the unreal thing. I take pictures which is kind of like making movies. And you made things up in your head." I stop. Do you say made or make to a ghost?

"Make," says Charlie, smiling a little.

"*Make*. I do that."

"Something else, Witch Baby." I wonder if he has curly toes. But he says, "I was by myself a lot too. I played the pain game."

So am I going to end up like him, alone and losing it because I don't find Angel Juan? I wonder. I remember the made/make thing. I hope he can't always read my mind.

"You don't have to," he says. "End up like me." Oh well for secrets.

All of a sudden I wish he was real. I wish he was my real grandfather or even my almost-grandfather but alive with his heart beating and sending warmth through his body—warmth that would turn into hugs and those plays he wrote. I wish he could pick me up and hold me. I'd smell coffee and cigarettes on his collar. We'd eat hot cinnamon-raisin bagels together and walk all over the city. I'd play my drums for him. He'd make everything okay.

"Do Mallard and Meadows know about you?" I ask.

"They are very nice gentlemen but they ignore the ghost closest to them."

"They'd get a kick out of you. Right in this city. In their building."

"They travel all over but this city is full of its own surprises," Charlie says. "Things pop out of the darkness like elves and fairies in a rotten wood or ghosts in a ruined house. I could show you if you want, the way I showed Weetzie and Cherokee." His voice cracks on their names and his face fades a little in the mirror.

"I am here to look for somebody," I say.

"Well you've found me. And I've found you."

"No. I mean I'm here to look for my boyfriend Angel Juan. He went away and wrote me one letter and . . ."

But Charlie twinkles out of the mirror—a light again.

"Charlie?"

The light disappears inside a crack in the old leather trunk.

I try to open the trunk—tugging at the straps and wedging my gnawed fingertips against the buckles. It's still all locked up. Charlie is gone.

❤

What a slam-a-rama dream!

But it wasn't. Or I'm still dreaming now. Because the first thing I hear when I wake up at almost noon is that singing again. This time it's "Witch Baby, Baby" to the tune of "Louie, Louie": "We gotta go now."

Go where? "Charlie?"

The light is by the window. "Take a picture," he says.

"Of what?"

"Of me."

I reach for my camera and focus on the light. But through the lens I see all of Mr. Bat again like in the mirror. He is looking out the window at the gray day, one bony hand pressed against the cloudy glass. He's so so thin, his jacket and pants just hanging on him like if you dressed one of my charm-bracelet skeletons in a suit. He turns and grins at me but only with his mouth not his eyes. His shoulders are hunched like two people at a funeral.

"Do you know how many versions of 'Louie, Louie' there are? It's unbelievable. Hundreds. No one knows what the real lyrics are."

Oh.

"You don't have much to eat here," he says.

"You eat?"

"No, but it's the idea. Like when I used to write about people traveling in space and battling monsters. We should go out."

"I'm going to go look for Angel Juan in Harlem today. He wrote me that he ate breakfast there."

"Sylvia's is in Harlem. That was Weetzie's favorite. Come on," Charlie says on the other side of my camera lens. "How often do I have the chance to watch my grandchild eat breakfast? Sweet-potato pie. Grits."

Maybe it's him calling me his grandchild or the grits like in Angel Juan's card or maybe just his moons-before-the-rain eyes but how can I not go with Charlie Bat? I put down my camera and he's a light again, ready to lead me out into the city.

We go down into the subway. It's so different today. Charlie—he's a dazzle at my shoulder like rhinestones splitting up the sun—whispers in my ear which way to skate.

An old woman with a shopping cart full of fish and bursting flowers made out of bright-colored rags.

She's sitting on a bench sewing like she's in her living room or her little shop, sewing fast like she can't stop, more and more tropical finned flower fish and exotic polka-dot flowers, like if she stopped the subway would turn real.

Three boys with guitars. One has a blonde bristle flattop, one is small with a long braid, one is tall with brown skin and ringlets. They are all wearing white T-shirts, torn jeans, steel-toed boots and strands of beads and amulets—peace signs, ankhs, crystals, scarabs. Their music reminds me of what Angel Juan and I heard in Joshua Tree. Celestial. Turning the subway into an oasis or a church. I wonder if they have wings, matted feathers folded up under their T-shirts.

A little farther along the air shimmers with the silver steel drum slamster sound. Some Rasta men with long swinging dreadlocks play. Makes my whole body ache for my drums for the first time since Angel Juan left.

The train comes, biting up the music. They should make subway trains that sound like steel drums.

Charlie and I get on. No music here or flowers or

fish. I hang on to the hand rail feeling my skate wheels roll at every stop and start like they want to take off, slam me down the aisles. What if I let go and let them? Would anybody even look up?

I use one hand to look at Charlie through my camera. He's sitting next to me jiggling his legs. The woman on the other side of him sneers. I guess she thinks I'm taking her picture. She's already growly 'cause I wouldn't let her sit in Charlie's seat. Charlie starts to whistle like trying to calm me down.

What song is it? Not "Rag Mop."

"'Papa's gonna buy you a hummingbird,'" Charlie sings. I don't think those are the right words. But the way he sings them is like a real grandfather would to a baby they love.

Harlem.

One thing good about Charlie being a ghost and not a guy is he can keep up with me on my skates and I'm jamming through the crowds of people like a hell bat. I feel like the whitest white-thing around except for Charlie, and he's a vapor.

I remember how I always wanted to slip inside of Angel Juan's brown skin. It seemed safer than mine. Now especially.

The sky is still gray and flat like stone, but when we go inside Sylvia's, sun pours through the windows. Sylvia's is warm and glinty with tinsel and it smells like somebody's kitchen.

"I brought Weetzie here," Charlie says.

"You talk about her a lot," I say. A woman at the next table rolls her eyes at her friend and I remember who I'm talking to and cough.

"She ate everything on the whole menu. And she was such a skinny bones. I don't think her mother fed her properly when she was growing up. How is she, Witch Baby? What's your life like now?"

I whisper so nobody takes me away for talking to myself. "We built a house in the canyon out of windows we collected. We play music and make movies. We eat a lot. Vegetarian. Weetzie's happy I think mostly. She misses you though."

"I wish I had talked to her about more things before I died. She shouldn't be missing me so much anymore. It's been a long time. But I miss her too," he says. "Maybe it's my fault."

The waitress comes over. I wish I was her color—maple-sugar-brown, darker than Angel Juan. And I wish I was big like that. The kind of body people want to snuggle with, not dangle on a plastic bracelet with other dancing skeletons.

"Yes?" the waitress says.

My stomach feels scratchy like it's filled with gravel so I just order coffee.

"That's it?" she says. "A little white child coming all the way to Harlem just for coffee?"

"That's it?" says Charlie.

"I'm not hungry."

"Not hungry? At Sylvia's? Smell." I can almost see Charlie sniffing the air like when Tiki-Tee sticks his nose out the window of Angel Juan's pickup truck on the way to the sea.

I remember what he said about the idea of eating. And the air does smell like browning butter and maple. "Okay, okay. I'll have eggs, grits and sweet-potato pie," I say. I look at the spark of Charlie-light. "Is that enough for you, Mr. Bat?" The waitress cocks her head at me and squints.

It's the best breakfast I've ever had and my stomach feels better. Every once in a while I pick up my camera to see Charlie. He's sitting across the booth dreamy in a halo of breakfast steam, his eyes half closed.

The waitress comes over to bring the bill and fill my coffee cup. She looks at me different for a few seconds, thinking. "You okay?" she asks.

I want to show her a picture of Angel Juan but they are all ripped up so I just say, "I'm looking for somebody. A cute Hispanic boy? He dresses like this." I am wearing my hooded mole-man sweatshirt with the hood sticking out of my leather jacket and a red bandana around my head.

"That sounds familiar." The woman squints again, this time at the shine of sunlight on tinsel which is really Charlie. "He liked my grits."

Angel Juan's card is in the pocket next to my heart. The part about the grits and how I eat like a kitten dipping my chin. "That's him," I say.

"Well, a lot of people like my grits. If it was him he hasn't been here for a few weeks."

She walks away. I wish I had on sunglasses. I can

tell my eyes are turning darker, bruise-purple with tears I won't let escape. It's like all of a sudden Angel Juan is so close and more gone than ever.

But the waitress stops and turns around. "There was one thing kind of strange." She looks at me and shrugs like, *This child talking to herself in my booth won't mind strange.* "He had leaves in his hair. I told him and he laughed and said it was 'cause he was living in the trees."

Living in the trees. "Come on, Charlie."

Outside.

It's overcast again. I look for trees where Angel Juan might be living but there aren't too many around here.

I skate past the Apollo Theatre and Charlie whistles for me to stop. I look into the glass of the ticket booth, Charlie reflected next to me. He takes off his top hat, rests it on his chest and bows his head.

"I used to make pilgrimages here from Brooklyn when I was a little boy. I wanted to move in," he says. "All the greatest of the greats played the Apollo. James Brown. Josephine Baker dressed up like a chandelier or a peacock. Weetzie's mother was always dressing up in things like that when I met her. And then Weetzie started with the feathers."

I look at the theater. I try to imagine the music steaming out and the people rushing in, the dancing, sweating, the lights like jewel rain glossy on everybody's skin. But it just looks like a run-down theater to me. I wonder if Angel Juan saw the Apollo, if he felt sad or if he could imagine everything the way it was. Maybe he doesn't need me around to see beauty the way I need him to see it.

"Charlie, I need to go now."

Some little girls are sucking on pink sticky candy and playing hip-hop-hopscotch in front of the theater to the ghetto blaster blasty blast.

"That might make a good picture," Charlie says.

I hold up my camera not really planning on taking anything. But through my lens I see they are mini flygirls with skin like a dark pony's velvetness. They are doing the Running Man and Roger Rabbit, Robocop and Typewriter in the chalk squares. There is something so complete about them. Like they don't need anything or anyone else in the world. I wish I felt like that.

"Go ahead," Charlie says.

I take their picture and they give me dirty looks at first but then they start getting into it showing off their moves.

"Hey," they say. "Hey. Yo." And I snap more and more hip hop-hopscotch shots. Sometimes I can see Charlie workin' it in the background looking kind of gawky and funny and rhythmless trying to dance with them.

"You going to make us famous?" one of the girls asks.

"Maybe so," I say.

After a while they stop and stand around me. They're as tall as I am. One stares at my hair.

"You could have some white-girl dreads if you wanted," she says. My hair is so tangled it does almost look like dreadlocks sometimes.

"What are you doing up here?" another says.

I've forgotten for a little while. It was so cool watching them. "I was looking for somebody."

"Can you dance?"

I look down at my feet in the roller skates.

"Any kid who can skate like you can dance,"

Charlie says. "Come on, Witch Baby."

I give him a grumpy scowly scowl. But the girls are waiting with their arms crossed. I take off my skates, hand one of them my camera and hip-hop into the chalk squares while Neneh Cherry raps on the ghetto blaster. The girls jump around laughing. When I get to the end of the hopscotch I do it backwards. I feel better. I feel almost free.

"Miss Thing! Now you can forget Homes, girl-friend," one of the girls says, giving me my camera. "He'll come back on his own. Just get yourself some tunes and a piece of chalk."

I put my skates back on. "I'll send you the pic-tures."

One of the girls writes her address on the back of my hand.

And I skate away, Charlie next to me, leaving them hip-hopscotching like maybe the next funky Josephines.

By the time we get downtown it's dusk.

"I want to go look in the trees," I say.

"We'll look tomorrow," says Charlie. "It's too dark now. Are you hungry?"

"Charlie, I ate all that food before."

"Witch Baby, that was hours and hours ago and you danced a long time. This is the best market in town."

"Were you always so into food?"

He's quiet for a minute doing dips and circles in the air like a firefly. "Actually no. But if I were to do life again I'd probably enjoy everything a lot more. For instance, I never used to dance."

I could have guessed that. "Weetzie said you were kind of a grumpster."

"Grumpster? Maybe. You learn things."

The little market has piles of fruit out in front lit up so they almost don't look real. Inside, the market's warm and bright and jammed with single people buying their dinners. There's a wild salad bar with Christmas lights all around and flowers frozen in the ice between the food. Charlie is flickering from the rainbow pastas to the stuffed grape leaves, from the egg rolls to the greens, between the beans, seeds, nuts, cheese, dried figs and dates and pineapple, muffins, corn bread, carrot cake, pastel

puddings, fruit, cookies. He wants me to get everything but I just take a pink sushi roll and a fortune
cookie.

In the window of the store next door there are
things like huge ostrich eggs and snakeskins and
skulls. I press my face up to the glass to look at a
human skull, trying to imagine what my own skull
looks like inside my head and what Angel Juan's
looks like and if our bones look the same.

"Thoughts like that will mess you up," Charlie
says in my ear. I keep forgetting about this mind-
reading thing.

We cross the street to get to the subway. But I see
a boutique—all chrome with high windows—and I
want to stop. Boy and girl mannequins in black
leather are kneeling around a man mannequin. He's
wearing a white coat with the collar turned up and
white gloves. He has white hair and pale no-color
glass eyes and girl's lips.

I feel so cold. I feel like one of those flowers in the
salad bar frozen in ice. But I don't want to move away
from the window.

"Witch Baby," Charlie calls. "Come on." His

voice sounds nerve urgent. Maybe that mannequin freaks him out too.

"You have to be careful," he says. "There's some nastiness around."

We go down into the subway where the noise and the dark are better than that plastic face.

"How does it taste?"

"Good."

"I mean really how does it taste?"

I am eating my pink sushi roll on the carpet at Charlie's place by the light of the globe lamp. I sigh. I wish he'd just let me alone to think about Angel Juan's bone structure.

"Seaweed, sesame, spinach, carrot, radish sprouts."

"Witch Baby, remember I'll never get to eat another thing."

"Okay okay." I close my eyes to get the tastes better. "The avocado's silky and the rice is sweetish— that might be pink sugar or something. The ginger's got like a tang. The horseradish burns right through my nostrils to my brain."

"Thank you," he says. He sighs like he's just eaten a big meal.

Later he goes, "What about dessert?"

I crackle open my fortune cookie and slip out the strip of paper from the tight glazed folds.

Make your own wishes come true.

Oh, really helpful. I crunch the cookie in my mouth and spread out the fortune so Charlie can read it. I sit cross-legged on the carpet.

"Do you believe in genies?" Charlie asks.

"Genies?"

"Weetzie tried to tell me once, something about three wishes and a genie? I believed in my monsters but not creatures that take care of you and grant wishes."

"Weetzie says people can be their own genies," I tell him.

"Well, you do look like a genie child to me. What would you do if you were a genie?"

Make Angel Juan come back.

"I think if you were a genie you'd live in your globe lamp and you'd ride this carpet everywhere taking pictures. You could get some pretty amazing shots from a magic carpet. You could go to Egypt and take pictures of kids riding the Sphinx. In Mexico you'd take pictures of kids in Day of the Dead masks running through the graveyards. And in exchange for letting you take their pictures you could grant their wishes."

That doesn't sound too sludgy. But it would have to be me and Angel Juan together.

Charlie laughs his crackle laugh. It reminds me of the sound of me eating the fortune cookie. "You should see yourself sitting there cross-legged," he says. "You look about to take off. Is there a mirror in here?"

We both look at the broken pieces.

"I was never into mirrors either," he says.

"Now you're *only* in mirrors."

"Maybe you could put that one back together again so you could see me. Don't you have some glue with you?"

I roll my eyes. Is he a clutch or what? How is gluing a mirror together going to help? But I get the glue from my bat-shaped backpack, pick up all the pieces from the mirror and start sticking them to the wall like a big starburst thing. It takes a while. Charlie whistles the theme to *I Dream of Jeannie*. Mr. Goof.

I look into the glass. Like that—all close together—the pieces break me up into a shattered Witch Baby the way I wanted last night.

"But you're not," Charlie says. "You're all one Witch Baby. And you are very beautiful, you know."

And there he is hovering just a little above me in the pieces of mirror. I think about the mannequin in white and Charlie calling me away, twinkling ahead of me as we went down into the subway dark.

"Good night, Witch Baby," Charlie says. He leaves the mirror, turns back into light and flash-dashes into his leather trunk.

"Good night, Charlie." My voice echoes—ghosts of itself—in the empty room.

I wake up to horns honking, tires screeching, snarling and yelling in the street.

At home Angel Juan and I used to wake up to the tartest summer-yellow smell of lemons and the whisper of the slick lemon leaves and the singing birds in the tree outside the shed. We named the birds Hendrix, Joplin, Dylan, Iggy, Ziggy and Marley. But here I haven't heard a bird the whole time. Not even a Boone bird or a Humperdink bird or a Neil Sedaka bird.

I want to go someplace where there are trees today. And mostly a boy living in the trees.

"I'm going to the park," I say.

"I took Weetzie and Cherokee to the park," says the only sunbeamer in the city flying out of the trunk in the corner. He always has to talk about Weetzie and Cherokee, Weetzie and Cherokee.

But then he says so soft and sweet, like he's talking to Josephine Baker or Weetzie or something, "May I escort you?"

In Central Park the trees are scratchy from winter. But they are trees at least. I follow the paths for a while—Miss Snarly Skate Thing—while Charlie flies around in the branches—Star Helicopter on Speed.

"Weetzie loved it here," he says. "It was spring. Weetzie took Cherokee running with her in a stroller. I thought they were like the flower goddesses bringing spring to the city. I couldn't keep up with them. Weetzie thought that kids who grow up seeing the world from a running stroller would be less anxious."

I wish Weetzie had taken me running in a stroller through Central Park with Charlie panting behind us, probably wearing his oxfords, baggy pants, his shirt-tails flying out. The world rushing by. Flowers in our hair. Leaves on the trees then. Ducks in the pond that's frozen now. People rolling on the grass 'til their jeans turned green. Maybe I wouldn't have shredded fingernails now if I had been in that stroller with Cherokee.

It looks more fun up there where Charlie is and easier to see what's happening so I take off my skates, hide them in between some roots and shimmy up.

"Where'd you learn to do that?" he asks from the branches. Mr. Flash.

"I've been climbing since I was little."

"*Since* you were little? What are you now?"

"You know what I mean."

"Since you were knee high to a grasshopper? A rug ratter? A baby witch baby?"

Where does he come up with this stuff?

"Aren't your feet cold?"

Is he kidding? My curly toes are furling up even more than ever in my socks. "Yes."

"Do you want to go back and get some shoes?"

"No."

I can almost hear him shrug. "Well, you could probably get some good shots from up here."

I look through my lens and there's Charlie perched on a branch clutching with his fingers. He doesn't seem too at home. He lets go for a second with one hand and points to the ground.

A woman with a baby on her back is looking through a trash can. The light is chilly and the color of lead. Even if I had color film it would be this black and white.

"Are you going to take a picture of her?" Charlie asks.

I dangle my legs and freezy feet over the branches and look down at the path. The woman is going through another trash can. I hold up my camera and she looks different all of a sudden. Or maybe it's just 'cause I feel different looking at her. I feel hungry, dizzy with hungry, sick with hungry even though I had breakfast this morning. I take my lunch—the loaf of French bread and the piece of cheese wrapped in a clean red bandana—and toss it

77

down. It lands on the scraggly grass by the woman's feet. She turns and picks it up, peeks inside and slips it into her jacket like she doesn't want anybody to see and then she goes away with her baby. I press my face against tree bark feeling the rough edges ridging my skin.

I follow Charlie over a bridge of branches into the next tree—a small gray one. I feel strong holding on to the limbs full of sap like blood. I think about lanka love goddesses with lots of arms. I want to hold on forever.

"Have you ever seen a tree spirit?" Charlie asks me and I shake my head.

"But I've thought about them. I used to look at trees and try to make up what their spirits were like."

"If you were one you'd be the spirit of those Weetzie-trees—you know, the ones with the purple flowers that get all over everything in the spring in L.A? They fell in the T-bird when the top was down but my little girl liked it. She said it made the T-bird like a just-married-mobile."

"I bet the spirit of this tree is an old woman—real smart—who talks to the squirrels and the moon," I say. I want him to come back, pay attention to me.

"Hey," Charlie says. "Look. Way up there."

I don't see anything.

"Through your camera."

In the highest branches a pair of legs swing back and forth. A woman with bird bones and skin like autumn leaves. She blinks her milky opal-sky eyes. Then she's gone.

Did I see that?

"You were right," Charlie says. "What about that one?" He points to a big muscle tree.

"A warrior dude with a hawk nose and raven-wing hair."

Just when I say it I spot somebody through my camera in the strong tree. A dark sleekster guy with tangly snarl-ball nests full of birds on his bare chunkster shoulders. He disappears into the top branches.

"Pretty good," says Charles.

"Let's follow him."

I have to go down on the ground to scramble back up into the next tree, and by the time I get there tree man is gone. Then I see something dangling in the branches hidden by the few leaves that are still clinging on. It's a rope ladder slinking from a square cut in some wooden boards. I hoist myself up behind Charlie into a serious kick-down tree house.

There's a rope hammock and an old cracked piece of glass fit into one window. And around the window frame somebody started to carve rough roses.

The kind that you carve on picture frames. The kind that Angel Juan's father taught Angel Juan to carve.

I feel like I'm still on the rope ladder. I feel like I *am* a rope ladder trembly in a wind storm. I grab onto the hammock but it swings and I stumble against the tree house wall. A ghost is here with me and I've seen two tree spirits, but finding this is the most slam-minest thing of all.

Angel Juan told me that someday he would build a tree house for us in the lemon tree looking out over the canyon. And the lady at Sylvia's told me that a boy who loved her grits and wore a mole-man sweatshirt and a bandana had leaves in his hair and said he lived in the trees.

"Charlie," I say all shaky. "We have to stay here. I have to wait for him to come back."

"It's too cold to stay here now. You don't have any shoes on."

"I don't care. He was here."

"If he was here I don't think he's coming back, Witch Baby."

"What are you talking about?"

"None of his things are here. And it's too cold."

I sit on the splintery floor of the tree house. I want to live here with Angel Juan. We could just go down to play music and make a little money, buy some food and come back, stay here all the time. In the spring we'd eat raspberries and kiss right in the hug of the branches, the stars shifting through the leaves like sparkles in a kaleidoscope. We'd wake up to a neighborhood of birds' nests right outside and the world far away down below. Sometimes Charlie Bat and the tree spirits would come over for dinner— or to watch us eat dinner I guess. We'd hardly ever have to leave.

I pick up a dried leaf and an acorn, with its little beanie cap, lying on the tree house floor. I try to bend the leaf to make it into an elf's coat for the acorn head but it crumbles in my hand. I look down through cracked glass at the winter park, the scattered people with maybe nowhere else to be.

Everybody should have their own tree house. Maybe Angel Juan and I could help build houses in every tree. If the tree spirits wouldn't mind. If I ever find Angel Juan again.

Someone is standing under the house looking up. Who wears white in New York City in the middle of winter except for maybe mannequins in store windows? All of a sudden I feel frosty, stiff and naked like a winter branch.

"Who's that?" I whisper to Charlie.

"He doesn't look like a tree spirit," Charlie says.

I swing down the rope ladder into the lower branches to see better but the snow-colored-no-colored man has disappeared.

I feel Charlie behind me. "I think we should leave now," he says.

On the way home Charlie stops in front of a glassed-in courtyard with a big twinkling tree, little tables underneath, heat lamps all around.

"What are those lights in the tree?" I ask.

"Fireflies."

"Fireflies in New York City? They look like a whole lot of guys like you."

"Let's go in and eat," says Charlie.

I don't feel like eating. I want to pad around in a circle on the carpet at Charlie's place like Tiki-Tee making his bed in the dirt and then I want to curl up there and sleep and sleep and have at least one dream about melting into Angel Juan. But I follow Charlie anyway. Maybe because Angel Juan and I used to eat samosas bursting peas and potatoes at an Indian restaurant in L.A. that looked like a camera on the outside. Maybe because of the fireflies.

I sit near a heat lamp that takes the cold ache out of my knobby spine. A man with incense-colored skin and a turban comes over. He has a liquid-butter voice. Ghee they call it on the menu he gives me.

Charlie tells me to order saffron-yellow vegetable curry with candy-glossy chutney, rice and lentil-bread. The food is so hot it scalds the taste right out of my mouth but it's so good I keep eating to get the taste back again. When I'm finished I stop to look through my camera at Charlie. He seems like he rocked on watching the meal about as much as I did eating it.

"Do you think that would make a good picture?" Charlie asks, pointing.

"Maybe *you* should start taking pictures." I'm sick of him telling me what to take all the time. "I want to go home now." But I look. Of course I look.

Across the courtyard are two tall beautiful lankas and a little girl. The little girl has red pigtails and freckles, wide-apart amber-colored eyes and gaps between her teeth. She looks just like one of the lanks. She keeps getting up from her chair and running around the tree squealing at the fireflies. The lankas take turns chasing after her, catching her, hugging her and sitting her down again, trying to get her to eat her rice. There is something about the three of them eating their dinner under the firefly tree that burns inside of me more than the food burning my mouth. They keep touching each other and laughing, sharing their tandoori chicken.

The red-haired lanka notices I'm staring at them and she smiles at me. She has the same gap-tooth grin as the little girl. Her friend gets up to catch the little girl who is off in another firefly frenzy.

I'm feeling sort of high from the hot food. "Can I take your picture?" Usually I don't ask—just do it—but it seems like with them I should.

"It's okay with me." Her voice is deep and rich like the ambery color of her eyes. "Honey," she says to the other one, "she wants to take our picture. Grab Miss Pigtails."

The friend has black hair and a diamond in her nose. She comes back with Miss Pigtails squirming in her arms. That squirmy-wormyness reminds me of me when I was little but I never giggled like that.

The lankas put their arms around each other and the little girl wriggles in between them still giggling. Through my camera lens I see their love even more. It's almost like a color. It's like a firefly halo. I also see that one of the lanks is beautiful in the strong way that only real androgynous ones are. She has really broad shoulders and long muscles and glamster legs. She laughs with a deep voice and if you look close you can see an Adam's apple.

I think one was probably once a man. That little

girl's mom was probably once her dad. But it doesn't matter because she is about the happiest kid I've ever seen.

"I'll send you one if you want," I say. I don't want to take any more pictures of them. I feel like maybe I saw a little too much.

But they're just smiling like they don't mind what anybody sees or thinks. They give me their address on a book of matches and I get up to leave.

The little girl is off again firefly chasing.

She points up into the trees. "I want one."

I would like to catch some too, put them in a jar. Put the jar in the tree house so Angel Juan would be able to read at night when he and I live there in the spring.

The red-haired lanka kneels next to the little girl. She plays with her pigtails and says, "They'd die in a jar. But you can have them all the time in the tree." The little girl looks into her eyes and nods.

I look through my camera at the firefly tree. For just a second I think I see a ghost-a-rama—a whole bunch of them, like they jumped out of some black-and-white movie except for their sparkly golden eyes—sitting in the branches.

I am huddling in a corner holding my letter thinking about being right where Angel Juan was living and not finding him.

Charlie is doing spin-dive-dips in the air and humming that song "Green Onions," trying to make me laugh but I don't want to laugh. I wish he'd just shut up and go back into his trunk. I want to think about Angel Juan. How we went surfing 'til the sun set on a beach where the sand was all polished black rocks. I cut my feet on the rocks and he put Band-Aids on them. We were changing out of our bathing suits behind the truck and saw each other naked under our towels and climbed into the back of the pickup truck and didn't leave 'til morning. Angel Juan pretended the salt water he dripped onto my cheeks when he kissed me was from the ocean but I knew it was his tears.

Finally Charlie settles on the trunk, stops humming and says, "Tomorrow I want to take you to the place I was born. I never got to take Weetzie there. I think about it all the time."

"Charlie, I have to find Angel Juan. I'm not here on vacation."

"Well, where are you going to go look?"

"I wanted to go to Coney Island but I think it's closed in winter."

"I can get you in. And I grew up right near there. We can stop on the way back."

This is the train to Coney Island. This is the darkness roaring around me that seems like it will never end. This is what it might be like to be dead.

And then the train comes up into the light. And everywhere for as far as I can see are hunched gnome tombstones. I think about what my tombstone will look like. Wonder if I'll be buried next to Angel Juan.

This is the darkness again.

This is the light.

This is Coney Island.

"I used to work here when I was a kid," Charlie says. "I learned how to run the Ferris wheel." He shows me a hole in a fence and we sneak through— well I sneak, Charlie's light just kind of glides.

An amusement park in winter is like when you go
to the places where you went with the person you love
but they're not with you anymore. Everything rickety
and cold and empty. If you had cotton candy it would
burn your lips and cut your throat like spun pink
glass. If you rode the roller coaster you'd have to hold
on tight to the bar to keep your whole body from being
lifted right off the seat with nobody there to hang on
to you except maybe a ghost. You used to always want
to go fast—speed monster—faster than anybody but
now if you rode the roller coaster you'd just keep
wishing for it to be over. The bathroom is filthy, stinky
so you don't go, and you have to walk around holding
it in. The booths are empty. No fur beasties for sale.
Why are you here? You remember the card in your
pocket. Your friend the ghost wants to cheer you up
and runs the Ferris wheel while you ride it all by
yourself thinking about the one on the West Coast
where you and your pounceable boyfriend made the
cart you were in swing and swing while you kissed
and kissed above the ocean and the pier and the
carousel, drenched in sunset, lips salty with popcorn
and sticky sweet with ice cream, not sick at all. This

Ferris wheel is different. Here you are on the most coupley kind of ride in the world all by yourself. You never knew you were scared of heights before. You just grip the bar and wish you were down. If you thought you were empty inside from being alone you know that you for sure have a stomach anyway but it doesn't want to stay in there. You also for sure have a heart which is beating hard and doesn't want to stay where it is either. You look down trying to think about something else and you can see popcorn bags, scarves, mittens and some rotting stuffed beast-ies in the weeds below where they must have fallen when the wheel turned last summer. You hold on tight to the card in your pocket and the angel around your neck and the camera in your lap. You remember how the card said that thing about riding the Ferris wheel to get outside of yourself. You try to look out over the park and up into the sky. You try to get outside of yourself to someplace where you don't feel so alone. The carnival booths are not tombstones, you tell your-self. But you think about the tombstones you saw from the train and how Charlie Bat is really dead and Angel Juan is gone. Then the plastic skeleton bracelet slips off your wrist. You watch it fall down into the thing-graveyard under the Ferris wheel.

When the ride is over you and the ghost go down to the weedy muddy slushy place and grope around in the dirt. You kick and pick through some stuff and after a while your friend spotlights the string of skeletons all quiet in the weeds. You pick them up and they start to shimmy, and underneath them you see what you probably most want in the whole world—or a picture of what you want most in the whole world anyway: his face three times in black and white. The boy you love caught in three photo-booth clicks. He looks very serious and older. And something else. There's a man sitting next to him. You can only see the man's mouth and chisel chin and his white shirt— the rest of him is cut off. You wonder who the man is and how you could have found this and what it means. You look into the dark of your angel's sunglasses like they are his eyes trying to see clues but there aren't any. You put the strip of pictures of his face into your pocket along with the card.

You see a photo booth and for a second you have the crazy thought that the boy whose face is in your pocket three times might be in there, sitting behind the dark curtain waiting for the shot.

You throw back the curtain with a negative of his smile flashing behind your eyes. But it's empty.

You sit down. "This is where Weetzie and Cherokee and I took our picture," says the ghost. "Maybe you could send her this one." He sits next to you reflected in the glass but you both know there will just be empty space when the photo comes out.

Three. In one you smile sickly sweet as cotton candy. In one you grimace like a little grumpster demon. In one you are just you—Witch Baby—looking straight out at yourself.

This is Brooklyn. This is the station and these are the people walking with their heads down and their hands in their pockets.

The rows of brownstones all look kind of the same at first until I notice the little piece of lace in a window, cat on a piano, the Big Wheel bike on the front step, the raggedy dead geranium plant waiting for spring. Some bearded guys in long black coats and fur hats walk by separate from the rest of the world like prayers in a book. Kids playing basketball, slammin' the way kids do, into it, not thinking about anything except the game. Pregnant teenagers with strollers.

I think about what it would be like if I had got pregnant with Angel Juan. Brown baby twins with curly cashew nut toes and purple eyes. Kid Niblett and Señorita Deedles. With no dad now.

Charlie's been quiet this whole time. Now he goes, "Would you like to see how it was?"

"Charlie, I just want to go home," I grunt. "Every time I get closer to Angel Juan you want to take me off in some other direction."

"I'm not taking you in any other direction. You tell me where we should go next."

"I don't know!"

"We'll go home soon. I really want to show you this. Over here."

He turns onto an empty street, looking like a sunbeam that decided to hang out a little longer than the rest. It's creepy-quiet and I wonder where everybody is. The sky is starting to get purplish.

"Look through your camera," Charlie says.

I look. But instead of him I see this little boy wearing short pants, bruised knees sticking out. He's black and white, shadows and light like Charlie.

"This is me when I was a kid," he says in a kid's voice.

"How'd you do that?"

"It's one of the things I can do now. Like climbing trees and walking through fences and dancing."

I hope he can't read my mind about the dancing.

"Besides, I used to be a special effects man," he says. "Come on."

I cross the street and stand next to him in front of a chunkster brownstone with dead rosebushes clinging to the sides. One time Angel Juan and I stole roses from the neighbors' gardens and put them on a cake we made but nobody would eat the cake because they were afraid of the bug spray (not 'cause of the stealing—they thought we asked) so we ate it all ourselves and got high maybe from the sugar or maybe from the bug spray or maybe because it was our special secret stolen thing.

Charlie points to a window on the top floor.

"That's where we lived when I was growing up."

"Hey, Charlie."

I turn around and hold up my camera. A little girl is standing in the street but she's not a real little girl. She's like Charlie, like her own movie without a projector.

"That's my sister Goldy," I hear Charlie say. He runs over to her and they start throwing a shadow ball back and forth. Then after a while I hear somebody calling their names from the window. I can't see anything but a champagne-colored glow until I hold my camera up and then I see the flickery face of a woman.

"That's my mother." Charlie's voice clicks a little. "She makes hats."

Charlie and Goldy run inside the building and I follow their echoing laughter upstairs into a deserted apartment that looks like nobody but maybe skulky rats have lived in for a long time.

"Look through your camera," Charlie says.

The apartment changes. It's suddenly warm and full of ghosty chairs and couches printed with cabbagy roses, crochet blankets, lamps with slinky silk fringe. There's a table covered with laces and ribbons, a sewing machine and a bunch of mannequin heads wearing huge hats decorated with flowers, fruits and vegetables, tiny birds' nests, butterflies, fireflies. I can smell onions cooking. The door opens and a man comes in. He's tall and his eyebrows grow together making him look kind of scary.

"That's my father," Charlie says to me. "He came from Poland on a ship when he was a little boy. They couldn't understand his name so they put down 'Bat' because of his eyebrows. His father was a fisherman. In Poland in the spring they filled their cottage with lilacs and covered the floor with white sand."

Charlie's dad goes over to where Charlie's mom is setting the table with china plates and he puts his arms around her. She pushes him away like playing but he spins her and lifts her up onto his wing-tip shoes and starts dancing with her like that, two grainy black-and-white images twirling like they got bored of staying inside their movie.

"Not tonight." Charlie's mom is out of breath. "It's the sabbath. Now stop that." She tries not to giggle.

Charlie and Goldy dance too, like the ghosts in the haunted house at Disneyland. Angel Juan's favorite. He wanted to dance in the ballroom with me and see if the ghosts would go through our bodies.

"Now stop," Charlie's mom says.

She pulls away from their grinning goofster dad and straightens her apron. She goes over to the table and puts a piece of lace on her head. Everybody else sits down while Charlie's mom lights some candles. She says a prayer with sounds from deep inside her throat. Then she serves baked chicken, peas, carrots and pearl onions. I've never seen a movie that smells this good.

"We light the candles for your grandparents in a few days." Charlie's mother passes a loaf of braided bread.

"When does the angel visit?" asks Goldy.

"Elijah doesn't come until Passover," Charlie's father says.

"And he'll drink the wine out of Papa's cup," says Goldy.

"Maybe someday Charlie will write a play about angels," Charlie's mother says.

"Charlie just writes about monsters," Goldy says. "He scared me again today, Papa."

"It was just a mask." Charlie holds up a rubber monster face. Goldy screams.

"Charlie, don't scare your sister," his father says. "Your mother's idea is good. You could write something about Elijah."

Charlie whispers to me, "The candles we lit once a year for the dead didn't mean much to me then. Until my mother got sick and then she died and the candles meant something and nothing at all. I decided when I grew up I wouldn't fast, light candles for the dead or pour wine for angels since none of it helped her stay alive."

Then he gets up from the table and goes over to his mother. He throws his arms around her all of a sudden so clutch tight. Even though he's a kid he's almost bigger than she is.

"Charlie?" she says. "What is it, *bubela*?"

Charlie just keeps holding on. Then he kisses her cheek, lets go and sits down again.

"They're all gone now," he whispers.

I look at Charlie's hat-making braided-bread-baking beautiful phantom mom. I think about how it must have been for him when she died. And for his sister and his father with the bat eyebrows. Now they're all dead. And I feel like it's hard for me to unclutch Angel Juan!

The Bat family is starting to fade. So is all the furniture in the room and the dinner smells. I press my eye to my camera trying to keep the picture but it's almost all gone. And then it is—gone. Just a deserted apartment about to be filled with night.

"Charlie!" I almost shout. Scared he's going to leave with them. I put down my camera searching for the light. "I'm sorry. I'm sorry I didn't want to come here with you." I look at the photo booth strip of me and not-Charlie.

Then, "Over here, honey," calls a voice from the doorway. Honey like salt in my throat making me want to cry. He's here. "We'd better go," he says.

We're back in the Village. I am sitting on the floor eating a rice cake.

"Couldn't you put something on that thing?" Charlie says. "It tastes—I mean it looks like you are eating cardboard."

I shrug. "I like it plain."

"You're getting so skinny."

Because I want him to enjoy my meal a little I go and get some peanut butter.

"Charlie, how did you deal when your mom died?" I ask.

"I wrote. I was okay as long as I was writing. Whenever anything hurt me I wrote, but after a while I couldn't anymore. I just stopped. It was like the sadness stopped filling me up with stuff to turn into art. I was just empty."

"That's how I feel."

"Make yourself keep taking pictures and the pictures will start filling you up again. And isn't there something else you like to do? Come on."

We go out of his apartment into the silent, shadowy hall. It seems like nobody else even lives in the whole building. We start down the stairs.

That's when I hear them. There on the eighth floor. The drums.

The sound makes me want to play so bad I have to stop and chew my nails. It's African drums in waves breaking again and again taking me out of my body.

A door is open and inside lit by pale winter sun from a big window dancers move in tides toward the drummers. The dancers wear batik sarongs—burnt-orange skies, jade-green jungles, violet-blue flowers —and shell belts that shiver on their hips. Their feet beat the floor like hands on a drum and their hands are bound by invisible ropes behind their backs, then turn into birds as they leap free. There are two little girls, and a woman with braids to her waist and a high dark gloss queen's forehead holds their hands and leads them down the room, her solid feet talking each step so that even though the kids probably just started walking a little while ago they are getting it. The drummers are men with bare chests and rainbow ribbons around their muscly arms. Some have dreads. Everybody in the room is sweating like it's summer and the music is setting free their souls into the air so I feel like I can almost see them.

All I want to do is play drums. I know the dances from when my dad filmed some African dancers and I got to jam with them.

When they take a break Charlie says, "Go ask him."

"I can't."

"Go on. How often do I have the chance to hear my witch baby play drums!"

Why do I listen to this crazy ghost? I don't know. My witch baby.

I go over to the head drummer—a tall man wearing full batik pants. His dreadlocks must be as old as he is, thick and wired with his power. I feel like a pale weasel baby staring up at him.

"Can I sit in?" I ask.

He looks down at me frowning like, *How can this will-o'-the-wisp white child think she can hang with this?* "Can you play?"

"I know *Fanga, Kpanlogo, DunDunBa, Kakilamba* . . ."

He raises his eyebrows. "This is a fast class. If you're not good it will be bad for everybody."

"You're good," Charlie whispers.

"I'm good," I say.

The man's still frowning but he points over to a little drum. It's perfect. A little heart of the universe.

They start again and it's a dance to heal sick spirits. The women throw spirits out of their chests, tossing back their heads with each fling of their hands. Their backs ripple like lanky lizards while their arms reach into the air and pull the healing spirits down into them. It's my favorite dance and so strong that while I play the drum I feel pain smacked out of me.

When the class is over the head drummer shakes my hand in his big callused hand. Him doing that is like having a medicine man pull out any other evil spirits that might be left over.

Charlie is waiting at the doorway, a pulsing golden light. "Yes!" he says. "Phenomenal. You are a beautiful drummer!"

I feel glowy all over, almost as bright as he is.

We go outside. I look up at Charlie's building. I wish I could take off the front of it and look into all the rooms like you do with a dollhouse. From out here it seems almost deserted like you'd never guess that magic-carpet-collecting ghost chasers live here and a whistling ghost in a top hat and that dancers and drummers are flinging bad spirits out of their bodies in one of the rooms.

I just wonder what my bad spirits look like and where all the flung-out bad spirits go.

All up and down the avenue shivering junkies are selling things. Ugster vinyl pumps, Partridge Family records, plastic daisy jewelry, old postcards. Where do they get this stuff? It's a magpie Christmas market.

"Look at that man," Charlie says.

I see a hungry face.

"No. With your camera."

I look through my camera at the man and I can almost feel the veins in my own arms twitch-switching with wanting. In a way the junkies aren't so much different from me or maybe from everybody.

I guess in a way Angel Juan is my fix and I've been jonesing for him. If he were a needle I'd be shooting up just like these jittery junkies. I'd be flooding my veins with Angel Juan. When we made love it felt like that.

And doing it can be about as dangerous as shooting up if you think about it.

And I wasn't the only one sad and lonely and freaked. There was a whole city of people. Some had to sell other people's postcards on the street just to buy a needle full of junk so they wouldn't shatter like the mirror I smashed with a hammer in Charlie Bat's apartment.

"Hey," the man shouts, "I've got something for you."

The man's sunken eyes are like Charlie's. I go over to his table and he holds up a pair of droopy soiled white angel wings. I touch the medallion in the hollow of my neck and think about the saint parade Angel Juan wrote about in his card. The little girls in feathers. I want those wings.

"How much?"

"Ten dollars."

"Five," Charlie whispers.

"Five."

"Eight and I'll throw this in." He waves a wrinkled postcard in front of his face. It has a picture of two Egyptian mummies on it. They remind me of my walk with Angel Juan when we saw the head of Nefertiti-ti on the piano in the window in the fog once upon time. I wonder if that king and queen ever screamed at each other and cried in the night with pain and desire or if they always looked so sleek and lazy-lotus-eyed.

I give the man eight dollars I was going to spend on food and he stuffs the bills into his pocket and licks his lips like he's already feeling what it's going to be like when the needle hits the vein. He could be a writer like Charlie Bat or a painter or a musician. He could have a kid like Charlie had Weetzie. And all people see is a junkie selling lost wings.

I flip over the postcard and it's like the dream I keep waiting to have but better because it's real. Is it real? Those slanty letters scrunching up toward the bottom like all of a sudden realizing there's no more space. I know those letters.

It can't be.

But there it is—his name.

Yo Te Amo, Angel Juan.

Dearest Niña Bruja,

I go to the museum and look at the Egypt rooms. The goddesses remind me of you. There are jars with cats' heads that hold the hearts of the dead.

This city is like an old forest or house that you

think's just rotting away and then you see there's magic inside. I try to remember that about life and about my heart in me. I think by being by myself I am learning how to love you more and not be so afraid.

Yo Te Amo, Niña,

Angel Juan

"Where did you get this?" I ask the man, almost screeching.

"I don't know. Found it."

"Where did you find it?" I growl, pulling feathers out of the wings.

He shrugs. Then he says, "Somewhere down on Meat Street. It was lying in the gutter like somebody dropped it on the way to the mail."

"Meat Street?"

"The meat-packing district. Somewhere around there."

I know I'm not going to get anything else out of him. But here in my hand is a postcard from the Metropolitan Museum addressed to Witch Baby Wigg

Bat, stamped, ready to be mailed and written by Angel Juan Perez.

I know where I'm going tomorrow.

I slip the postcard into the pocket next to my heart with the other card and the photo booth strip, sling the wings over my shoulder and try to skate the shakes out of my knees. Charlie twinkles near my ear like a whistling diamond earring.

Today Charlie and I go up the steps where people from all over the world are huddling in their coats with Christmas shopping at their feet. They're eating hot dogs and salt-crystaled soft pretzels. The pretzels smell good. Buttery, doughy. But I'm not going to spend any money on food today even though Charlie keeps telling me I am too skinny and I have to eat.

We go into the big entry that's high and bright like a church. Perfume and flowers. Voices echo. Warm bodies. Cool marble.

Egypt first.

There is so much here I feel like, How am I supposed to even start? Rooms and rooms of glass cases.

Mummies. Real bodies inside there. High lotus fore-
heads. Painted tilted fish-shaped eyes. Smooth flat
jewel-collared chests. Lanky limbs. Long desert feet.
I bet inside they don't look like that. Jars with the
heads of baboons or cats or jackals for holding the
organs like Angel Juan said.

Cases and cases of tiny things. Secret scarab
beetles. Why did the Egyptians have this thing
about dung beetles? Mud love. Sludge and mud. It
reminds me of me when I was a little kid covering
myself with dirt. Slinky cats with golden hoops in
their ears. Chalky blue goddesses missing their little
arms or legs. Where did the lost parts of them go?
Maybe they reminded Angel Juan of me because
they're broken.

"You know, you look like a little Egyptian queen,"
Charlie says. His reflection ripples like water next to
mine in the glass case.

We come out of the dim tomb rooms and at first I
can't see—it's so flood-bright. The glass walls let in
the park and the ceiling lets in the sky. And in the
center is this whole temple—this huge white
Egyptian palace with the lotus-head people carved on

the sides and a shallow pool of water all around full of penny wishes.

Charlie sighs. "This was Weetzie's favorite place in the whole city. She did like the dancing chicken in Chinatown too."

Could you please stop bat-chattering about when Weetzie visited you.

I think it and I don't even care if he can read my mind.

"I'm sorry, Baby. I'm trying not to be such a clutch pig. Isn't that what you say? A lankster lizard?"

I sit down on a bench facing the temple and pretend that I'm in Egypt. I wear a tall headdress, a collar of blue and gold beads and a long sheer pleated tunic. I pray in a gleamy white temple. I ride on the Nile in a barge and play drums. I carve pictures of my family on stone walls. I have a slinkster cat with a gold hoop in its ear that sits on my shoulder and helps me understand mysteries. When I die I'll be put in a tomb and my organs will be put in jars. If somebody finds me centuries later they will know exactly where my heart is.

On the way back through, Charlie leads me into a

tiny room. Nobody else is here. I'm blind after the brightness of the temple. The darkness feels like it's seeping into me, drugging me like spooky smoke, mystery incense taking me into an ancient desert.

Then I see the hipster king and queen from the postcard standing together with their organ jars next to them, staring out at me like, *Hello, we are perfect twins and who are you?*

"*Hello, we are perfect twins and who are you?*"

"Did you say something, Charlie?"

"Not me."

"Well don't tell me *they* said it." I lower my voice, hiss-whisper. "Charlie, what's going on?"

"Maybe you should introduce yourself."

"Oh *right*. Okay. My name is Witch Baby. I shouldn't be surprised that statues are talking to me. I've already seen tree spirits and my best friend almost-grandpa is a ghost. This is Charlie."

"*Hello, Witch Baby. Charlie.*" Two voices—a drum and a flute, one song.

I look at the pair of statues with their matching smooth golden faces, high eyebrows, far-apart eyes, small noses, graceful necks. Part of me wishes that

that was me and Angel Juan—together forever with our hearts in jars. Better than not knowing where his heart is.

No. Shut your clutch thoughts up, Witch Baby. You don't wish that.

"You are alive. Remember. As long as you are alive you'll know where his heart is. It will be in you."

"Like Charlie will always be alive in Weetzie and me?"

"Yes."

"Charlie, did those statues really talk to me?"

"I'm not in a good position not to believe that, being myself a . . . well you know. Anyway, you heard what you needed to hear. Maybe I did too.

"Shall we try China?"

In China there is a room full of beamy-faced people doing yoga. They make a wreath around me, flower children breathing peace. The Egyptians were so much in the world with all their gold and stuff but these guys are like from some other world. They don't have wings but they remind me of angels.

In a room with a high ceiling I stand at the solid feet of a massive Buddha dude. His stone robes are

covered with petals and they fall like silk. His hands
are gone. I wonder what happened to them.

He has a topknot, droopy earlobes and a gentle
mouth. He is gazing down at me like, *Everything will
be all right, Baby, no problem.*

"Everything will be all right."

"Charlie!"

"If any statue could talk it would probably be
him. Why don't you ask him something?"

"Why are your earlobes like that?"

"Witch Baby, that might not be the best ques-
tion."

"Well it's hard to think."

*"I used to wear big earrings when I valued material
wealth."*

"What am I supposed to do about Angel Juan?"

"Let go."

All of a sudden I know just how his hands would
be if they were there. One would be held up with the
thumb and third finger touching and the pinky in the
air. One palm would be open.

Next Charlie and I go to Greece. In the airy echoing room of dessert-colored marbles we stand in front

of a pale boy, so beautiful on his pedestal but so white. The marble muscles mold marble flesh. There are even marble tendons, ridges of marble veins, so real they look like if you pressed on them they'd flatten out for a second. I wonder how the real boy who posed for the statue felt. If he felt like the statue took his soul away, like all that mattered was his pretty body.

The statue seems to be looking at me like . . .

Yes, it's happening again:

"Your friend needs to go make music by himself."

"You mean he needs to not just be my pounceably beautiful boyfriend who I take pictures of and write songs about."

"Yes."

"It might be even hard for him to be made into stuff by me until he starts making stuff of his own."

"Yes."

I take the strip of photos out of my pocket and try to look into Angel Juan's eyes behind the sunglasses.

While I'm standing in front of the pedestal boy looking at Angel Juan I hear something behind me.

"Do you wish that you could turn him into stone? Make him a mummy? Keep his heart in a jar?"

Another talking statue? But this time the voice makes me feel cold like marble. I turn around.

No statue but that man—the one in the white coat, the one from the park.

He slithers behind a wall painted with flower garlands and demon masks.

I run after him.

"Witch Baby!" Charlie calls.

I don't stop. My footsteps echo through the rooms. The blank eyeless marble eyes are all around.

But when I get to the lobby the man is gone and I am still marble-slab cold.

"Who was that ghoulie guy?" I ask the Bat Man back at the apartment.

"I don't know," he says. "But you shouldn't go chasing after that kind of people. Maybe you should take some pictures."

"Of what. Of you?"

"I'm not very photogenic. You're going to take pictures of you."

"What?"

115

"Look in the trunk."

I jiggle the lock and the leather trunk opens right up. I choke on stink-a-rama mothballs and dust.

Inside is a bunch of stuff. Clothes. Wigs. Masks. I figure either Charlie got off dressing up weird when he was alive or they were for his plays. Either way the trunk is filled with stuff to make me into all my dreams and all my nightmares.

I turn into Nefertiti in a gold paper headdress and collar with cool kohl eyes and a pout of my lips.

I wear a curly blonde wig, a wreath of plastic leaves and a toga sheet and do a Greek-dude-statue-on-a-pedestal thing.

I keep on the wig and attach the magpie-market wings to my back for a Cupid look holding a rickety bow and arrow from the trunk.

I put my hair in a topknot and wear an old silk kimono and be Buddha cross-legged and meditating.

I find a really ugster monster rubber monster mask. I don't even want to touch it. It looks like some leper-monster's shed skin all shreddy at the edges. Just like the one Charlie had in Brooklyn. But I put that on too and take a picture of my face with the eyes staring out of two holes gouged in the rubber.

I slick back my hair, put on my dark glasses, bandana, hooded sweatshirt, leather jacket, Levi's and chunky shoes.

Me as Angel Juan.

Click. Click. Click.

I stay up all night. The sky is starting to get pale.

The black top hat that Charlie was wearing when we first met is in the trunk too and I put that on with a black tuxedo jacket, dark eyeliner circles under my eyes: the ghost of Charlie Bat.

"Do I look like you, Charlie?"

"You are a lot like me, especially the way I used to be. Even without the costume. You're more like me than Weetzie and Cherokee. I think you are my real blood granddaughter."

I wonder if he knows how slink that makes me feel. How I feel warm for the first time since I've been in this city, I mean really warm. From the inside out.

I hear his crackly voice. "We both believe in monsters. But all the ghosts and demons are you. And all the angels and genies are you. All the kings, queens,

Buddhas, beautiful boys. Inside you. No one can take them away."

"So then that means nobody can take you away from Weetzie and me even though you're—"

"Yes, I guess you're right."

Why doesn't he let me finish?

"You should get some sleep now," he says.

Suddenly I'm so tired. I collapse onto the carpet with all the costumes all around me.

Dear Angel Juan,

I dream about you for the first time since you left. You are wearing the magpie-market angel wings and standing on a street corner playing your guitar, singing for a crowd of people. You look so happy and free.

But who's that? There is someone hiding in the crowd watching you that shouldn't be there. Someone in the rubber monster mask from Charlie's trunk. They want you to belong to them. They want to lock you up in a tomb so you can't breathe, so no one else can ever touch you, so you can't sing anymore.

I wake up with a cold. One of those bad almost flu-y things where you feel all your nerve endings splitting on the surface of your skin and your ears ring like you've been playing a tough gig at a loud smoky club all night. I've slept for hours—it's dark. When I go to turn on the globe lamp nothing happens. I try the bathroom switch. Nothing. Electricity out. And you know what it is? Christmas Eve.

In Los Angeles my family is all together feasty-feasting in a house lit with red and green chili-pepper lights. There is a big blazing tree. After they eat they are going to make home movies of each other dancing and opening their presents.

I wish I was home with all of them and Angel Juan having a jammin' jamboree, playing music and sharing a stolen-roses cake in front of the fireplace.

"Charlie?" I say.

No song. No light.

I light candles and wrap up in my sleeping bag and some of Mallard and Meadows's blankets on the carpet. I remember that my heart is a broken teacup.

I remember the feeling of my own heart shredding me up from the inside out. I think about the dream.

"Charlie!"

"Are you all right?" he asks flickering in a corner.

"I had a bad dream about Angel Juan. I have to go out and look for him." I try to stand up but I have Jell-O knees.

"You look like you have a fever," Charlie says. "You can't go out."

"But Charlie, I think that man in the museum wants to hurt Angel Juan."

"Just rest now, Baby." His voice is like a lullaby.

I feel creepy-crawly. I shiver back into a fever-sleep.

When I wake up this time my skin feels sore—like it's been stretched too tight or something—and hot. Outside the firefly building is shining in the night.

Then I remember my dream again and I feel splinters of ice cracking in my chest. Now what? All I know is that I have to go out no matter what Charlie thinks. I'm so sick of him telling me what to do, keeping me from finding Angel Juan. And he's hiding in his trunk now anyway. There is something I have to do.

I get up and dress in baggy black. I put my hair back under a black baseball cap, grab my camera and roller skates.

When I get down to the street I put on my skates and take off into the darkness. My hands are frozen inside my mittens and my frozen toes keep slamming against the pointed cowboy-boot toes. My nose is running and my chest aches. Fog is coming in and the air smells salty and fishy. A few glam drag queens in miniskirts and high heels are strutting in the shadows cooing and hollering. Sometimes a car drives by, stops and picks one up.

It's freaky. I kind of know exactly where I'm going. Or I don't know but the roller skates do. They just seem to carry me along over the cobblestones. I can feel every stone jolting my spine but not enough to jolt the fear out of me. Driving it deeper in.

The place where the roller skates want to take me is the meat-packing district down by the river.

Meat Street, I think, remembering what the junkie said.

In between the big meat warehouses on the cobblestone pavement is a little fifties-style hot-dog-
shaped stainless-steel diner-type place lit with tubes
of buzzing red neon that make the shadows the color
of raspberry syrup. The neon sign reads "Cake's
Shakin' Palace."

And standing there in the window of the empty
diner is Angel Juan!

I think it is really him. Not so much because I feel
tired and spooked and sick but because I just want it
to be. I want him to be all right.

But this is a mannequin. It has Angel Juan's
nose and cheekbones and his chin, his dark eyes
and hair and even the tone of his brown skin under
the raspberry-syrup light. He's dressed like a waiter
with a white shirt and a bow tie and a little cap and
there's a tray with a plastic milk shake and burger in
one hand. I am standing here on a dark street in New
York in the middle of the night in front of a window
looking up at my boyfriend offering me a hamburger
but his body would be cold if I touched it and if I held
a mirror up to his face no breath would cloud it. His
eyes are blind. But for some reason I have the feeling

that this really *is* Angel Juan. I can't explain the feeling except that it is the scariest thing I have ever felt. I think I will be sick right here on the street, dry heaves because my stomach is empty.

Then I hear something behind me and I turn around shivering like somebody just slid some ice inside my shirt down my spine. There's this guy standing there.

He is tall and he has white hair and you can almost see the blood beating at his temples because his skin is so thin and white. He has those eyes that look like cut glass and those pretty lips and he's wearing that white coat. He is probably the most gorgeous human being I have ever seen in real life and the most nasty-looking at the same time.

He's the mannequin in the boutique window and the man in Central Park and at the museum.

"It's kind of late for you to be here, isn't it?" he says. He has a very soft voice. Something about his voice and the dry sweet smoky powdery champagney smell of his cologne and the way his hands look in his white gloves makes me want to sleep. "I don't open for a few more hours."

"I was just kickin' around," I say.

He glances up at Angel Juan in the window of the diner. "Would you like something to eat?" he asks me. "You look hungry."

I know it is stupid to be standing here talking to this freaky beautiful man but somehow I can't split.

"I make great hamburgers." He smiles. His teeth look really yellow next to his white skin, which is weird because the rest of him is so perfect. "Or milk shakes if you are a grass-eating *vegetarian*."

This is his place—the diner. And in the diner is a mannequin of Angel Juan. So what am I supposed to do? I stand watching him take out a set of keys like they are something that a hypnosis guy swings in front of your face to put you to sleep and I follow him inside.

He puts on some lights and the spotless curved silver walls of the diner shine. The floor is black-and-white squares and the counter and swivel chairs are mint green. There are mirrored display cabinets on the walls full of fancy cakes that look like they are going to slide right down into your mouth. I feel a blast of sleepy heat filling the place.

"Sit down," he says. "What would you like?"

"I'm okay," I say. I don't want to eat but all of a sudden my stomach starts making noises like I haven't had food in it for weeks. Then I remember I really haven't eaten anything except some rice cakes in a while.

He smiles like Miss Shy Girl Thing. He goes behind the counter and takes off his gloves. I can see the blue veins in his hands. Then he starts scooping and mixing and whirring until he has made this amazing thick frosty snowy whipped-cream-topped vanilla milk shake. He puts it in a tall parfait glass, plops on one of those poison red candied cherries Weetzie won't let us eat, sinks in a straw and sets it on the counter. Then he presses raw meat into a patty and slaps that onto the sizzling grill. I haven't eaten a hamburger in a long time because no one at my house is into meat anymore but that meat smells pounce-able. I feel dizzy. I skulk over to the milk shake on the counter and take a sip. You know those cold-headaches you get from eating ice cream too fast when you are a kid? That happens. But the sweet milkiness is like warm kisses at the same time so I just keep inhaling on that straw even with my head and chest frozen and hurting.

The man finishes the hamburger, slides it onto a fat sourdough bun, adds lettuce and onions and a juicy slab of tomato, stabs the whole thing with a toothpick and sets it in front of me on a plate. I almost fall on top of it. I can taste the meat before my teeth plunge in.

The man puts on the jukebox and it plays "Johnny Angel." I am so drugged by my meaty hamburger that it takes me a while to realize that Johnny Angel and Angel Juan are the same song. Same name. The voice singing "Johnny Angel" seems to be laughing at me, the whole jukebox shaking with laughter like, *Look at this crazy girl following some stranger into his diner trying to save her boyfriend who isn't even her boyfriend anymore because of some weird creepster dream.*

This is how people die. This is how kids are murdered. This is how you lose your mind and then your body and maybe this is how you lose your soul. Johnny Angel.

The man puts on a white waiter's cap like the one Angel Juan is wearing in the window and he leans over the counter staring at me with his no-color eyes.

"I am Cake," the man says.

He looks up at the neon-rimmed clock on the wall.

"I'm late," he says like the White Rabbit in *Alice in Wonderland*, putting his gloves back on. "Come on. I have something to show you."

I don't know why I get up and go with him. But I keep thinking about my dream and the Angel Juan mannequin in the window.

Cake kneels on the floor behind the counter and lifts up one of the tiles. There's a dark staircase going down. Cake moves his hand for me to go first. Cake smiles and he looks like a guy in one of those sexy jeans ads but all bleached-out.

I hear music coming from down below and I think I recognize it. It sounds like the tune to "Niña Bruja," which is the song that Angel Juan wrote by himself when he was in Mexico. It has a kind of psychedelic sixties sound. I look up at Cake. Behind him, in the window of the diner, I can see the back of the Angel Juan mannequin's head.

Then I take off my roller skates and squeeze down through the trapdoor.

Cake follows me but it is more like I am following him even though I go first.

We walk down a few flights of stairs. Every once in a while there is a gold hand sticking out of the wall holding a neon candelabra with neon-tipped candles and you can see that the walls are red velvet but it is mostly pretty dark. I can still hear the music and I start to smell the sweet smoky smell, like what Cake is wearing only stronger and coming from ahead of us. I can feel Cake smiling behind me.

When we get to the bottom of the stairs there's a door. I can hear the music jamming louder now, making the door shudder but it isn't Angel Juan's song anymore. It still has a psychedelic sound though. Cake opens the door.

Here's this room with walls paneled in gold paint, mirrors and white velvet, white marble floors with red veins running through and huge red neon candles everywhere and all these kids sitting really still like statues. They are of all different races but they look kind of the same, I'm not sure why. They're all in white. All their eyes are really big and their cheeks are sunken and the girls look like boys and the boys look like girls. Then I realize they *are* statues like the mannequin of Angel Juan upstairs in the diner, which seems so far away now. One of these mannequins is sitting on a big overstuffed red velvet thing shaped like a mushroom and he's holding a long neon pipe. Real smoke is coming out of the pipe and filling the room and I wonder if the smoke is why I'm feeling drowsy. It smells like Cake. There're these other mannequins sitting at a long table. On one end is this guy with a really big droopy red velvet top hat that covers his eyes and at the other end there's this girl with white hair and buck teeth and in the middle of the table there's this huge teacup about the size of a baby bed which is what it is I guess because there's a baby mannequin sitting in it. Then there's a dark-skinned boy curled up on the floor and grinning so big and hard it looks like it hurts him even if he is a mannequin, which he is. The whole thing is too much for me and I think how I can get out of here when Cake comes up and puts his gloved hand on my shoulder.

"This is Cake's *real* shakin' palace," he says.

"What's your name, sweetie?"

I don't say anything.

"Are you a runaway?"

I shake my head. It's hard to talk.

He smiles, pressing his lips together and nodding like—*right*. "I see kids on the streets like you. It's a crime the way they live. I feed them upstairs and then we come down here to play. They're like my family." He takes off his white coat. He is wearing a white double-breasted suit. "Will you dance with me?"

Before I know it I'm letting him twirl me around. I feel like one of those ballerinas on music boxes going around and around like I can't stop. My baseball cap flies off and my hair snakes out. I want to stop but Cake is still twirling me. Finally I fall against his white suit. I have a flash of dancing with Angel Juan at my birthday party once a long time ago. Feeling so safe inside those arms. Nothing could hurt.

"Don't be afraid, little lamb," Cake whispers. Lamb. Angel Juan used to call me that. "You're home now. Cake will take good care of you."

When I wake up I'm lying in the softest bed hung with white silk. I might be dead. Everything is so soft and quiet. The whole room is covered in white silk.

I feel sore and muffled from my cold, which is a full-on flu by now. I try not to think about who put me in this bed. Then I remember Cake and the mannequin kids. I've got to get out of here.

That's when I hear the whistling. I have never loved that goofster song so much in my whole life. Whatever it means. "R-A-G-G M-O-P-P Rag Mop doodely-doo."

Charlie B., Chuck Bat, the Bat Man. The glowy glow is hovering like a hummingbird. I get up and reach for a huge heavy silver hand mirror by the bed.

And there he is looking at me and waving his hands around all frantic.

"What is it, Charlie?" I ask. "Are you okay?"

He's not okay. I mean even for a ghost. His eyes aren't just sad. They're like tormented. I think he wants to tell me something.

"Do you want to tell me something?"

He points at me, puts his finger to his lips, points to the door. Then he turns slowly in the mirror so his back is to me. Stuck to his back are the wings I bought on the street! He looks at me over his shoulder.

"Angel?" I mouth.

Charlie turns back around and points to his heart. Then he clasps his hands together. I think about the brother grip.

"Angel Juan."

Charlie puts his finger to his lips again. I look toward the door. When I look back there's an ugster monster in the mirror. It takes me a second to get that it's Charlie wearing the rubber monster mask from the trunk. He takes it off and looks at me with those crazed eyes again.

Charlie's face in the mirror starts to blur. Then he flies out of the mirror like a comet. Out the door. I follow him.

We go down a maze of red-veined white marble hallways that seem like they don't lead anywhere. We pass mannequins half dressed in silk flowers and vines, sitting on garden swings that swing back and forth from the ceiling. Blonde boy mannequins on skateboards balanced on marble ramps. A glittery girl with blonde cotton-candy hair and a wand like

Glinda's from *The Wizard of Oz*. A huge fish tank with mermaid mannequin children and tropical fish. A tall angel with a very young glowy face riding on a statue of a fish with plastic kids kneeling all around him. And somewhere, behind one of these doors we pass— my grandpa's ghost and me trying to be that quiet—is Cake sleeping with his pale eyes open. I hope Cake is sleeping. And maybe behind one of the doors ahead is Angel Juan.

I'm out of breath. I lean against the icy-veined marble wall and it makes my bones ache. I feel like I'm in a tomb. I wipe my forehead. My whole body is pounding with fever-fear.

Charlie's light is doing the nerve-jig so I keep following him through the maze and into a room made of mirrors. And there in the mirror, jiggling like a puppet made of light, like the plastic charm-bracelet skeletons, like a life-sized Day of the Dead doll, is Charlie. He waves his hands all excited, his face scrunched with worry, and I figure out he wants me to press on one of the mirror panels and it opens. Out of the mirror he turns into a light again and we go down a staircase. At the bottom is a metal chamber room.

It's so small and crowded with naked mannequins that I feel like I can't breathe, like the mannequins are hogging up all the air. A mannequin falls against me, hitting me with its jointed plastic arm and I look at its face and I see that it is Angel Juan. He's bald but it's him. I try not to scream but I jump back and bump into another mannequin and that one is Angel Juan too. I start slamming around and they're all falling on me and every single one has Angel's face. This is a room full of Angel Juans. What does this Cake want? What is happening here?

Then I notice the Charlie glow lighting up a corner of the room.

I touch the silvery angel that sleeps in the hollow part of my neck.

A boy is slumped against a wall with the mannequins all around him and a guitar with the Virgin Mary in a wreath of roses painted on it leaning against his chest. His hair is long and falling in his face and he looks like he hasn't eaten much in a while but even though he's changed a lot I know right away who he is. And it's like I understand stuff all of a sudden.

Dear Angel Juan,

*Do you know when they say soul-mates?
Everybody uses it in personal ads. "Soul-mate wanted."
It doesn't mean too much now. But soul-mates—think
about it. When your soul—whatever that is anyway—
something so alive when you make music or love and
so mysteriously hidden most of the rest of the time, so
colorful and big but without color or shape—when
your soul finds another soul it can recognize even
before the rest of you knows about it. The rest of you
just feels sweaty and jumpy at first. And your souls get
married without even meaning to—even if you can't be
together for some reason in real life, your souls just go
ahead and make the wedding plans. A soul's wedding
must be too beautiful to even look at. It must be blind-
ing. It must be like all the weddings in the world—
gondolas with canopies of doves, champagne glasses
shattering, wings of veils, drums beating, flutes and
trumpets, showers of roses. And after that happens you
know—that's it, this is it. But sometimes you have to
let that person go. When you're little, people, movies
and fairy tales all tell you that one day you're going*

135

to meet this person. So you keep waiting and it's a lot harder than they make it sound. Then you meet and you think, okay, now we can just get on with it but you find out that sometimes your soul brother partner lover has other ideas about that. They want to go to New York and write their own songs or whatever. They feel like you don't really love them but the idea of them, the dream you've had since you were a kid about a panther boy to carry you out of the forest of your fear or an angel to make love and celestial music with in the clouds or a genie twin to sleep with you inside a lamp. Which doesn't mean they're not the one. It just means you've got to do whatever you have to do for you alone. You've got to believe in your magic and face right up to the mean nasty part of yourself that wants to keep the one you love locked up in a place in you where no one else can touch them or even see them. Just the way when somebody you love dies you don't stop loving them but you don't lock up their souls inside you. You turn that love into something else, give it to somebody else. And sometimes in a weird way when you do that you get closer than ever to the person who died or the one your soul married.

———∞∞∞———

I run over and fall down next to him and put my arms around him and he looks up like his head is almost too heavy to lift and his jaw drops but he doesn't say anything. He almost looks as blind as those mannequins himself. But his heart is beating and he's not made of plastic and I have my arms around him. He is in my arms.

Charlie-light starts doing his nervous dance like he wants us to hurry.

I try to get Angel Juan to stand up but it's like he's too weak or something—he just slumps down again, his fingers catching in my sweater and bringing me down with him. I try to think of what to do but every time I see the plastic mannequin faces staring at me and the plastic smiles made from my boyfriend's lips and teeth I just go blank. I just keep thinking over and over again, What is Cake trying to do? How could this be? How can anything I do save us from this kind of a ghoulie demon-thing?

And then we hear something that sounds like glass shattering. For a second I think of how I smashed that mirror in Charlie Bat's apartment and how stupid that was and that I'll be lucky if I'm around long enough to get seven years of any kind of luck at all. And then before any of us can move, the Cake demon comes storming into the room, pushing over the mannequins. He has blood on his hand. Maybe he cut himself on the mirror he broke in the mirror room. The blood is so red against his white hand and dripping onto his white silk robe. It almost seems like he wouldn't have red blood because he is so white. Like he'd have white icing coming out of him or something. But it's blood. I just stare at it. Then I see that he's holding something wrapped in a sheet and his blood is getting all over that too.

"What are you doing down here?" he says in his very soft voice. "Who said you could come down here?" He is King Clutch Warthog.

"I was just kickin'."

"Well, it's all right," Cake says. "I have something for you anyway."

He starts to unwrap the thing he's carrying. I see that it's another mannequin and it's smaller than the

Angel Juan mannequins. I see the back of its head and it reminds me of the time when I shaved off all my hair with my dad's razor. Then I realize that the reason I'm thinking that is because this mannequin's head looks exactly like the shape of my head without any hair. Cake spins the mannequin around and there's me, Witch Baby—it's my face with the pointed chin and the tilty eyes. I hold on tight to Angel Juan's hand.

"When?" I say.

"I made her while you were sleeping. You've been sleeping for a few days. I'm going to put you inside of her."

"Why?" I say.

"Do you know about mummies? It's a little like that. I give you a place to sleep. All the children that I find. It's like you are immortal." Cake strokes the cheek of one of the Angel Juan mannequins. "Usually I just make one. But he is so beautiful. I just keep wanting to make more of him. Now I guess I'll have to put you both away for good." He looks at us with his pale-crystal eyes.

He comes toward me and puts out his hand—the one that's not bleeding. I want to go to him. I feel

139

drowsy. I wish I had the globe lamp Weetzie gave me to ward off evil.

But:

Believe in your *own* magic, Weetzie said. Maybe my own magic gave me Charlie Bat.

Look stuff right in the eye, Vixanne Wigg said. Look at your own darkness. Maybe Cake is that. Maybe Cake is me. The part that wants to keep Angel Juan locked in my life.

All the ghosts and demons are just you, Charlie said.

Look stuff right in the eye.

But I can't look in Cake's eyes. I'll be under his spell. So I take my camera and look at him through that.

My own magic. Maybe magic is just love. Maybe genies are what love would be if love walked and talked and lived in a lamp. The wishes might not come true the way you think they will, not everything will be perfect, but love will come because it always does, because why else would it exist and it will make everything hurt a little less. You just have to believe in yourself. Look your demons right in the eye. Set your

Angel Juans free to do the same thing themselves.

I snap a picture of creepster Cake with the last shot in my camera. There is a flash like lightning.

My wishes are: my beloved Angel Juan is free, Charlie Bat finds peace, Cake becomes who he really is. These are my wishes.

Cake starts to shake. He is a white blur. Then he gets very still.

Angel Juan's limp fingers wake up in my hand. "Niña Bruja," he says. I look at him. We are both crying like babies. I feel my fever break into clean sweat. Angel Juan takes my hand and presses it to his lips. We put our arms around each other in our brother grip. And we watch Cake seal up inside himself, becoming a bleached plastic mannequin man without a breath or a heartbeat. He's not any different from before really. This is who he really is.

We can leave.

Charlie's light leads us out of the chamber, down the halls. Angel Juan doesn't ask about the light that looks like it's coming from an invisible flashlight. He leans against me, holding my hand.

We get to the gold-and-white room with the mannequin smoking a pipe and the family having a tea party and the grinning boy. None of them will ever leave. They look so real that it seems like we could wake them and take them with us but I know if I shook one of them the only sound would be the clatter of bones against plastic. Angel Juan knows what I'm thinking. He holds my hand tighter as we go through the door that leads back to our life.

It's dark when Charlie, Angel Juan and I come up into the empty diner. The jukebox is still playing "Johnny Angel" like it never stopped. My dirty dishes are still on the counter. But the Angel mannequin isn't in the window anymore.

I put on my skates. We go outside and it's so cold that Angel Juan and I can see the ghosts of our breath on the air. We put our arms around each other in our perfect-fit brother grip. We stumble-shake-skate back to the apartment following Charlie's light.

If Charlie's building reminded me of a beat-up old vaudeville guy when I first saw it, now I think all the rooms are like songs he still remembers in his head.

And the best song is on the ninth floor in the Rag Mop room.

There is a note on the door.

> *Dear Lily,*
>
> *We are home. The ghost is at peace. We hope you don't mind but we let ourselves in to give you a few things. Come by as soon as you can. We are worried about you. Love from your benevolent almost-almost uncles, Mallard and Meadows.*

We go in. Charlie flies right over to his trunk and slips inside.

I look in the cupboards and the refrigerator. Mallard and Meadows filled them with food—apples, oranges, scones, bagels, oatmeal, raisins, almond butter, strawberry jam, tea and honey. Angel Juan and I chomp-down lap-up almost everything and fall onto the Persian carpet wrapped in each other like blankets.

"Thank you, Niña Bruja," he whispers, taking me

in his arms. "You set me free, Miss Genie."

His eyelids flicker closed and I can hear his breathing getting deeper. I get up and go over to the trunk.

"Come on, Charles," I say.

I look into the mirror pieces. "Grandpa Bat?"

Slowly, like when ripply water in a pool gets still so you can see yourself, his face floats up out of the murky murk of the mirror.

"I'll miss you, Witch Baby." His voice fortune-cookie crackles, old-movie pops.

"You can come back with me to L.A. Weetzie would rock."

"I can't."

"Well then I'll visit you."

"No. I'm going to leave now. I needed to finish some things and now I'm done."

"Finish what?"

"I wanted to stay and meet you, little black lamb. And make sure you would be all right. I wanted to help you but I messed up and really you helped me."

"You didn't mess anything up."

"I didn't help you find Angel Juan."

"You helped me find me. You helped me rescue Angel Juan."

"I guess I did. I did something right finally. Something besides Weetzie."

"What did I do for you?"

"You made me see how I was—what is it you guys say—clutching? Onto Weetzie. Onto you so you couldn't do what you had to do. Clutching on life."

"How did I do that? I just hung out with you. You're the one who showed me all around."

"I saw you learning how to let go. And I have to remember I'm not alive anymore, honey."

"What am I supposed to do now?"

"Take your pictures, play your drums. I should have kept writing my plays."

"Don't go away, Charlie."

"Good-bye, Baby. Send my love to everyone. Especially Weetzie. I love you."

"Charlie. Grandpa."

But Charlie Bat smiles. It is strange and slow-mo. Real peaceful like the Buddha. It seems like his eyes are smiling along with his mouth now for the first time, the pupils almost disappearing into a crinkle of lines, just shining out a little. He lifts his hand and waves it back and forth, long fingers leaving a trail of light. Then he disappears into the darkness like a candle blown out. The shiny restless whistling whirr of energy that was my grandfather ghost is quiet now. All I see in the mirror is a kind-of-small girl. Maybe she looks a little like an Egyptian queen.

I open the window and look out. Blast of cold air makes my snarl-ball hair stand up on my scalp. There are stars, electric light bulbs, candles, fireflies. There are a million flickers, glimmers, shimmers, flashes, sparkles, glows. None of them will sing "Rag Mop" to me. None of them will take me through the city. None of them will tell me that we have the same blood. But in all of them is some Charlie Bat.

"Good-bye, Grandmaster Rag Mop Man," I whisper, lying down to sleep next to Angel Juan.

Dear Angel Juan,

I dream we are inside the globe lamp. But this time we just sleep there for a little while like two genies. In the morning we will fly out of the lamp. We will be able to travel all around the world on our magic carpets, you and I, seeing everything—sometimes parting, sometimes meeting again.

It's almost the next night when we wake up, shy like we've never touched each other before or something.

I get the rest of the food and we munch it sitting on the carpet talking about the things we've seen. Angels and fireflies, temples and flea markets. How I found his photo booth pictures and his lost postcard. We don't talk about Cake though.

"I started playing my songs on the streets," Angel Juan says. "People give me money."

"Can I hear?"

And Angel Juan plays the song on his guitar.

Panther girl you guard my sleep
bite back at my pain with the edge of your teeth
carry me into the jungle dark
lope easy past the eyes that watch

stride the fish-scale river shine
and the pumping green-blood vines
we will leave my tears behind
in a pool that silver chimes
we will leave behind my sorrow
leave it in the rotting hollows
when I wake you are beside me
damp and matted from the journey
your eyes hazy as you try to know
how far down we tried to go
and the way I clung to you
all my tears soaking through
fur and flesh, muscle, bone
like a child blind, unborn
whose dreams caress you deep inside
are my dreams worth the ride?

In all the time we've made music together I have
almost never heard his voice by itself without the rest of
our band. It's a little scratchy and also sweet. I look at
him and think, he's not a little boy anymore. He can go
into the world alone and sing by himself. I am so hypno-

tized that at first I don't realize that the words are almost the same as the letter I wrote to him and never sent.

"How did you know?" I say when he is done. I am out of breath.

"What?"

"You just know me so much. How do you know me so much?"

He grins. "Do you like it?"

I don't have to say anything. He can see in my face.

"Baby, I missed you," he says.

"Do you need to stay in New York still?" I ask it looking right at him trying not to crampy-cram up inside.

He looks back into my eyes and nods. "I think so. A little while longer."

"Aren't you scared?"

"It's okay now. It's over."

It is.

"Maybe you could stay with me," he says.

"I have to go back to school and everything."

"Do you want me to go home with you?"

I look out the window. I think about Angel Juan playing his music down there in the streets. I think about

149

the crowds rushing past. Some of the people stopping. Breathing in his music like air. Feeling it warm their skin and take them to places where it is green and gold and blue. Taking them into their dreams. Suddenly they can remember their dreams and walk through the city streets wearing their dreams. They turn into panthers, fireflies, trees, fields of sunflowers, oceans, avalanches, fireworks. It's all because of Angel Juan and his guitar.

"No," I say. "You stay. You can stay in Charlie's apartment."

"Niña . . ."

I put my finger to his lips. They press out firm and full and a little dry against the pad of my fingertip. I can feel my own lips buzz.

"I don't think I should stay in your family's place," he says.

"Weetzie would want you to."

"Only if you ask her."

"Angel Juan," I say, "I found your tree house."

He looks at me, his eyes so sparkly-dark. "Niña," he says. "Only you could do that."

"Were you with anybody else?" I ask.

"No, Baby. I thought about you all the time."

"What about that thing you said about us being together just 'cause we're scared of getting sick."

"I'm so sorry I said that shit. It scared me that you were the only person I've ever loved like this."

"Who was that man?"

"He was our fear," says Angel Juan. "My fear of love and yours of being alone. But we don't need him anymore."

I feel the tight grainy cut-glass feeling in my throat and my eyes fill up. Crying for the mannequin children and how we had to learn.

"Don't cry," Angel Juan says, but it looks like he is too. "You'll get tears in your ears. Don't cry, my baby. You saved me."

Then I feel Angel Juan's lips on mine like all the sunsets and caresses and music and feasty-feasts I have ever known.

It's the best feeling I've ever had. But it's not the only good feeling. I kiss Angel Juan back with all the other good feelings I can find inside of me, all the magic I have found.

When we go downstairs to see Mallard and Meadows it's kind of late.

Mallard throws open the door letting out steamy, fresh-baked-bread-and-cinnamon-incense-air into the hall. "There you are," he says. "Meadows, she's fine."

"This is Angel Juan," I say as we come inside to the candlelit apartment lined with magic carpets.

Mallard and Meadows shake his hand. "Happy New Year," they say.

Happy New Year? Angel Juan and I look at each other. When did that happen?

"We lost track of time," I say.

"Well, it's New Year's," says Meadows. He smiles. "And Christmas too."

Mallard points to some packages. "They came for you in the mail."

We sit on the carpet eating cranberry bread while I open my packages.

There's film for my camera.

I take a picture of Mallard and Meadows on either side of Angel Juan in front of a wall with a magic carpet on it.

There's also a big black cashmere sweater and warm socks that I make Angel Juan take for himself.

From Weetzie there's a collage she made and put in a gold-leaf frame painted with pink and blue roses. The collage has pressed pansies, rose petals, glitter, lace, tiny pink plastic flamingos and babies, gold stars, tiny mirrors and hand-colored cutout photographs of my family. In the center there's a picture of me and a picture of Charlie Bat goofing in his top hat and it looks like we're holding hands. Something about our smoky eyes and skinny faces makes us look like a real grandfather and grand-daughter.

There's a letter from Weetzie too.

Dear Witch Baby,

Happy Holidays! We all miss you so much. We're sending you a ticket to come home on the second. I hope you have found everything you are looking for.

After you left I thought a lot about why I couldn't dream about Charlie. I think it was because I was

holding on and trying too hard. But somehow know-
ing you were in his apartment bringing new life there
I could let go of him. I realized how I miss you, honey,
and I can <u>see</u> you. Charlie's gone. I made this collage
of you and him and that night I dreamed about him.
He seemed very peaceful and happy in the dream and
it was so real.

I'm also sending you this other package that came
in the mail.

We are all going to be there to pick you up from the
airport.

We love you.

Weetzie

The other package is from Vixanne. I know right
away but I don't know how I know. I open it.

The girl is staring with slanted dark-violet eyes
under feathery eyelashes. Her hair is black and shiny
with purple lights, every strand painted so you can
almost feel it. Her neck and shoulders are bare and
small painted with creamy paint and there is a hum-

mingbird hanging around her throat. She's in a jungle. Thick green vines and leaves. You can almost hear the sound of rushing water and feel the air all humid. On the girl's left shoulder is a black cat with gold eyes. On her right shoulder is a white monkey with big teeth bared. The scary clutch monkey is playing with her hair. Perched on top of her head are butterflies with wings the color and almost shape of her eyes.

"It's you," says Angel Juan.

It's weird because I guess it really does look like me but I didn't recognize myself. The girl is strange and wild and beautiful.

I think about Charlie like the black cat and Cake like the white monkey and how they are both parts of me and about butterflies shedding the withery cocoons, the prisons they spun out of themselves, and opening up like flowers.

Angel Juan just puts his arms around me. Mallard pours all of us some sparkling apple cider.

"How was your ghost?" I ask.

"He's fine now. His daughter and he just had to let each other go. She had to believe . . ."

"That he's inside her?"

"In a way. You know, Lily, you might make a good ghost hunter someday."

I just smile and we clink our glasses watching the tiny fountains of amber bubbles.

"Happy New Year."

Outside the window is New York City with its subways and shining firefly towers, its genies and demons. It is waiting for Angel Juan to sing it to sleep.

I look at Angel Juan. My black cashmere cat, my hummingbird-love, my mirror, my Ferris wheel, King Tut, Buddha Babe, marble boy-god. Just my friend. I know I'll be leaving him in the morning.

At home I'll skate to school and take lots of pictures. I'll take pictures of lankas, ducks, hipsters and homeboys. When I look through my camera at them I'll see what freaks them out and what they really jones for, what they want the most in the whole world and then I'll feel like they're not so different from me. I'll send copies of my New York pictures to the hiphopscotch girls, the beautiful lanks and their Miss Pigtails, the African drum-dancers. I'll take more pictures of me too, dressed up like all the things I am scared of and the things I want. One will be of genie-me in a turban doing yoga next to the globe lamp with smoke all around me. Maybe Vixanne would like to see my pictures.

I'll play drums with The Goat Guys and write songs about New York and my family and me. I'll help with my family's movie about ghosts. I think they should call it *The Spectacular Spectral Spectacle*. It could be about a ghost of a man who helps a girl free herself from an evil demon ghoulie ghoul and how the girl lets go of her dad and sets *his* spirit free.

I might not see Angel Juan for a while. But we'll see each other again. Meet to dream-rock-slink-slam it-jam in the heart of the world.

Like we always do.

baby
be-bop

part one

Dirk and Fifi

Dirk had known it since he could remember. At nap time he lay on the mat, feeling his skin sticking to brown plastic, listening to the buzz of flies, smelling the honeysuckle through the faraway window, tasting the c̶ ̶ g of graham cracker cookies and milk in his mouth, wanting to be racing through space. He tried to think of something he liked.

He was on a train with the fathers—all naked and cookie-colored and laughing. There under the blasts of warm water spurting from the walls as the train moved slick through the land. All the bunching calf muscles dripping water and biceps full of power comforted Dirk. He tried to see his own father's face but there was always too much steam.

Dirk knew that there was something about this train that wasn't right. One day he heard his Grandma Fifi talking to her canaries, Pirouette and Minuet, in the teacup-colored kitchen with honey sun pouring through the windows.

"I'm afraid it's hard for him without a man around, Pet," Fifi said as she put birdseed into the green dome-shaped cage.

The canaries chirped at her.

"I asked him about what the men and ladies on his toy train were doing, Mini, and do you know what he said? He said they were all men taking showers together."

The canaries nuzzled each other on their perch. Pet did a perfect pirouette and Mini sang.

"I guess you're right. It's something all little boys go through. It's just a phase," Fifi said.

Just a phase. Dirk thought about those words over and over again. Just a phase. Until the train inside of him would crash. Until the thing inside of him that was wrong and bad would change. Until he would change. He waited and waited for the phase to end. When would it end? He tried to do everything fast so it would end faster. He got A's in school. He ran fast. He made his body strong so that he would be picked first for teams.

That was important—being picked first. The weak, skinny, scared boys got picked last. They got chased through the yard and had their jeans pulled up hard. Sometimes other kids threw food at them. Sometimes they went home with black eyes, bloody noses or swollen lips. Dirk knew that almost all the boys who were treated this way really did like girls. It was just that girls didn't like them yet. Dirk also knew that some of the boys that hurt them were doing it so they wouldn't have to think about liking boys themselves. They were burning, twisting and beating the part of themselves that might have once dreamed of trains and fathers.

Dirk knew that the main thing was to keep to himself and never to seem afraid.

Every Saturday afternoon his Grandma Fifi took him to see a matinee, where he could hide, dreaming, in crackling popcorn darkness. They saw James Dean in *Rebel Without a Cause*. That was who he wanted to be. He practiced squinting and pouting. He turned up

his jacket collar and rolled his jeans. He slicked back
his hair, carefully leaving one stray piece falling into
his eyes. James Dean was beautiful because he didn't
seem afraid of anything, but when Dirk looked into
his eyes he knew that he secretly was and it made
Dirk love him even more.

Grandma Fifi had two friends named Martin and
Merlin who were afraid in a way Dirk didn't want to
be. They were both very handsome and kind and
always brought candies and toys when they came over
for tea and Fifi's famous pastries. But as much as Dirk
liked Martin and Merlin he knew he was different
from them. They talked in voices as pale and soft as
the shirts they wore and they moved as gracefully as
Fifi did. Their eyes were startled and sad. They had
been hurt because of who they were. Dirk didn't want
to be hurt that way. He wanted to be strong and to love
someone who was strong; he wanted to meet any gaze,
to laugh under the brightest sunlight and never hide.

Dirk especially didn't want to hide from Grandma
Fifi but he wasn't sure how to tell her. He didn't want
to disturb the world she had made for him in her cottage with the steep chocolate frosting roof, the bird-

bath held by a nymph and the seven stone dwarfs in the garden. There were so many butterflies in that garden that when Dirk was a little boy he could stand naked in a crowd of them and be completely covered. Jade-green pupas hung from the bushes like earrings. Fifi showed Dirk the gold sparks that would later become the butterflies' orange color. Then the pupa darkened and stretched and finally a fragile monarch bloomed. Fifi and Dirk put flower nectar or a mixture of honey and water on their fingertips and the newborn butterflies crawled onto them, all ticklish, and practiced fanning wings that were like amber stained glass in the sun. In the garden there were also little butterflies that looked like petals blown from the roses with the almond scent. There were peaches with pits that also smelled and looked like almonds when you cracked them open. Fifi showed Dirk how to pinch the honeysuckle blossoms that grew over the back gate so that sweet drops fell onto his tongue. She showed him how to pinch the snapdragons' jaws to make them sing. If Dirk ever cut himself playing, Fifi broke off a piece of the thick green aloe vera plant she called Love and a gel oozed out like Love's clear, thick blood.

Fifi put the gel onto Dirk's cut and stuck a Peanuts Band-Aid over it; the cut always healed by the next day, skin smooth as if it had never been broken.

Fifi had a cat named Kit who had arrived through the window one evening while an Edith Piaf record was playing and never left. Kit had pinkish fur like the tints Fifi put in her white hair. If Dirk or Fifi ever had an ache or a pain, Kit would come and sit on the part of the body that hurt them—just sit and purr. She was very warm, and after a while the soreness would disappear.

"Kit is a great healer in a cat's body," Fifi said.

Kaboodle the Noodle was Fifi's dog. He had a valentine nose, long Greta Garbo lashes and a tiny shock of hair that stood straight up. When you were sad he kissed your hand and winked at you.

Dirk and Fifi and Kaboodle went shopping at the fruit stands on Fairfax that were covered with pink netting to keep out the flies. Kaboodle sat out in front and waited. Fifi bought bags of asparagus and bananas, kiwis and radishes, persimmons and yams. There was a little Middle Eastern market where she bought bottles of rose water and coffee beans as dark as chocolate. Fifi made pastries shaped like shells, ballet slippers and moons, and salads full of vegetables cut into the shapes of flowers.

Dirk knew that Fifi wanted great-grandchildren someday. She wanted to make pastries for them and teach them about how peach pits smelled like almonds, about butterflies that looked like flowers and about talking snapdragons. He knew he was her only chance. Worst of all, he knew she wanted him to be happy and how could he be happy in this world, he wondered, if what he knew about himself was true? So Dirk didn't tell Fifi. He didn't tell anyone. He kept to himself. He waited for the phase to end. Until the day he met Pup Lambert.

Dirk and Pup

The air smelled like lemon Pledge, sweet jasmine and mock orange. Bougainvillea grew thick up the fences like walls of paper flowers. Morning glories glowed neon purple, twining among the pink oleander. Nasturtiums shimmered along the ground like fallen sunlight.

As Dirk walked home from school he heard a whistle, and he looked up into an olive tree. In the branches sat a boy. He had brown hair with leaves in it, freckles on his turned-up nose and a Cheshire cat grin.

"Hey," the boy said.

"Hey," said Dirk.

"Want to shoot some baskets?" the boy asked.

"Sure."

The boy jumped out of the tree, landing lightly on the white rubber soles of his baby-blue Vans deck shoes.

Dirk and the boy shot baskets in the driveway of the pale yellow house with the pink camellias growing in front. Dirk was taller, but the boy was light on his feet and had perfect aim. Dirk's heart was beating fast like the basketball hitting the pavement again and again; he was sweating.

When a car pulled into the driveway the boy grabbed the basketball and took off down the street.

"Come on," he shouted.

Dirk stood still, looking at the boy and then into the car. A heavyset man got out. Dirk just had time to wonder how such a big man could have such a quick and slender son when the man said, "Scram! I told you not to hang around here anymore! I'll call the cops!"

Dirk ran after the boy. When he caught up with him, at the edge of a field of wildflowers, he was out of breath. The sweat was getting into his eyes.

"I thought that was your house," Dirk said.

The boy grinned. "Nope."

They stood under the shifting sunlight, laughing. Dirk thought their laughter would look like sunlight through leaves if he could see it. A flock of poppies, with their faces toward the sun, moved in the breeze as if they were laughing too. Dirk noticed that the boy's ears came to slight points at the top.

"I'm Pup," the boy said.

"Dirk."

"Hey, Dirk. Next time we'll borrow someone's swimming pool."

Two days later Pup jumped out of the tree again. He and Dirk climbed the fence of an ivy-covered Spanish house with a terra-cotta roof, and stripped down to their underwear. Then they took turns diving into the aqua water. Pup did more and more elaborate dives—cannonballs and flips and flailing-in-the-air things—and Dirk tried to imitate him. They stayed in the pool until the tips of their fingers looked crinkled and crushed, and then they dried out on the hot cement. Pup had freckles on his shoulders and a gold dusting of hair on his arms and legs. With his wet hair slicked back Dirk thought he looked like James Dean.

"Are you hungry?" Dirk asked Pup.

"Starving."

Dirk and Pup went to Farmer's Market where the air smelled like tropical fruit, chilled flowers, Cajun corn bread, Belgian waffles, deli meats and cheeses, coffee and the gooey sheets of saltwater taffy that spun round and round behind glass. The light filtered softly through the striped circus tent awnings. Wind chimes and coffee cups sang. Dirk looked for Pup but couldn't find him. Then he heard a whistle. He followed the sound to a corner table where Pup was sitting behind a huge banana cream pie. He handed Dirk a fork.

"Want some?"

"Where'd you get that?" Dirk asked.

Pup grinned his Cheshire grin.

Nothing had ever tasted so good to Dirk as that frothy concoction—peaks of meringue and melts of banana—that Pup had lifted so slyly from the pie counter. But the next day Dirk asked Grandma Fifi to make a pie so Pup wouldn't have to steal and invited his friend over for dinner.

After school they went to Fifi's cottage through the backyards of houses, leaping fences and climbing walls, patting dogs and dodging the lemons that one woman threw at them. Pup gathered avocados, roses and sprigs of cherry blossoms as he ran so that by the time he met Grandma Fifi at the front door he had almost more presents than he could carry.

"This is Pup," Dirk told her.

"Pleased to meet you, Pup," said Grandma Fifi. "Thank you for the alligator pears and the flowers."

"This is my Grandma Fifi," Dirk said.

"Hi," said Pup. He seemed suddenly shy. He shook the tips of his hair out of his eyes. He lowered his eyelashes.

"Come in for some snacks," said Fifi.

She brought out guava cream cheese pastries and a pitcher of lemonade. Pup gulped and swallowed as if he hadn't had food in days.

Then Dirk showed Pup the comics that he drew. They were about two boys who turned into the super-heroes Slam and Jam when there was danger.

"You're serious," Pup said.

They lay on the floor of Dirk's room reading comics until the room turned jacaranda-blossom-purple with evening and the glow-in-the-dark constellations that

Fifi had pasted on the ceiling began to come out.

"Superheroes aren't afraid of anything," Pup said softly, his voice fading with the light.

Kit jumped off the windowsill where she had been gazing at the blur of a hummingbird in the bottle-brush bush and sat on Pup's chest, over his heart. Kaboodle licked between his fingers.

"You don't seem afraid of much," said Dirk.

"I'm afraid of everything. That's why I do stuff. My mom is afraid of everything too but she just stays inside. She's afraid to go to the market, even."

"You can come over and eat with us when you want," Dirk said. "My grandma would like it."

"Thanks," said Pup.

He stayed for chicken pot pie with carrots and peas and peach pie for dessert. When you asked Fifi for pie you got it.

While they ate their dessert Fifi played an old record.

"Chills run up and down my spine / Aladdin's lamp is mine," the singer crooned, and Dirk felt silvery chills, saw, beneath his eyelids, the glinting lamp of love.

"This is cool music," Pup said.

"Do you dance, Pup?" Fifi asked.

"Not really," Pup said. "But I'm willing to have some lessons."

Fifi blushed. "Oh, I'm not very good anymore."

"That's not true," Dirk said. "She's a cool dancer."

"Show me," Pup said.

He stood and offered Fifi his hand. She took it, putting his other arm around her waist. Dirk watched as Fifi led Pup around the room so skillfully that it appeared he was leading her. But that was also because Pup was a natural dancer. Dirk watched how he held his head, proud on his straight strong neck, the way his shoulders curved.

"Your turn now, Dirk," Fifi said.

Dirk wasn't embarrassed the way he would have been around anyone else except Pup. Fifi felt light in his arms as they danced over the garlands of roses on the carpet. Pirouette and Mini did a waltz in their cage. Kaboodle sat up on his hind legs and offered Pup his paws. While Pup danced with Kaboodle, Kit watched them all from the mantelpiece.

When the record ended Pup insisted on skate-boarding home although Fifi tried to offer him a ride. He and Dirk planned to meet in the quad at school the next day at lunch.

That morning Dirk told Fifi he was especially hungry so when he opened his lunch there was one sandwich with cheese, avocado, lettuce, pickles, arti-choke hearts, olives, red onion and mustard and one with peanut butter, raspberry jam, honey, bananas and strawberries, both on home-baked bread.

"She always does that," Dirk said, pulling out the sandwiches and shaking his head. "Would you eat one of these, Pup?"

"Are you sure?"

"She acts all hurt when I bring one home but she keeps giving them to me."

Every day after that Fifi put two sandwiches in Dirk's lunch. She never asked her grandson why he had started to eat twice the normal amount. She just beamed at him and said, "You are growing so tall and strong. And so is your friend Pup Lambert. When I first met him I was sad to see how thin he was."

"I love you, Fifi," said Dirk.

"I love you, Dirk," Fifi said.

After school Pup and Dirk listened to music in Dirk's room. They could play it loud because Fifi was a bit hard of hearing. On the wall was a chalk drawing Dirk had made of Jimi Hendrix.

"That is hell of cool," said Pup. "You are a phenomenal artist, man."

Dirk tried to concentrate on keeping his ears from turning red.

"My mom went out with this gross trucker guy once," Pup told him. "He saw the Jimi poster in my room and goes, `That nigger looks like he's got a mouth full of cum.' I wanted to kill him. I told my mom I would if she didn't stop seeing him."

"Did she?"

"Yeah. But I don't think that's why. Her next boyfriend saw my Bowie poster and started calling him a fag. My mom said if I ever dressed like that she'd kick me out of the house."

Dirk and Pup looked up at Jimi burning his guitar. It flamed beneath the steeple of his hands, between his legs. Jimi had said it was like a sacrifice. He loved his guitar. He was giving up something he loved. Dirk wondered if Jimi had felt that way about life.

"We should start a band," Dirk said.

"Can you play?" asked Pup.

"A little. I mess around with my dad's guitar."

Dirk got out the guitar that he kept hidden in the closet.

Pup stroked it. Dirk had never seen him touch anything with such concentrated love except for Kit and Kaboodle. Just like Kit and Kaboodle, the guitar seemed to love Pup. Dirk imagined he could hear it singing in Pup's arms although Pup's fingers never touched the strings.

"It's beautiful," Pup said. "Your dad was cool."

"I don't remember him," Dirk said.

"What happened?"

"My mom and dad died in a crash."

Pup looked up at the picture Dirk had drawn of his hero standing with his hands in his jeans pockets, shoulders hunched, feet rolling out.

"Like James Dean?"

"Kind of."

Pup's eyes got big. "I bet your dad looked like

James Dean," he said. "'Cause you do."

Dirk picked up the guitar and bent to tune it so that Pup wouldn't see that his ears were turning red. He felt almost as if Pup had put his arm around him and said, "I'm so sorry about your parents, Dirk. I wish they were alive."

Pup took a cigarette out of his pocket.

"Where did you get that?" Dirk asked.

"I steal them from my mom."

He lit the cigarette and handed it to Dirk. Dirk hesitated. He didn't want Pup to see him cough like someone who had never smoked before.

"You know I still cough sometimes," Pup said as if he could read Dirk's mind. "And I've been smoking for a year."

Dirk inhaled. He could feel where Pup's lips had been, moist on the paper end. Pup was unscrewing one of the large brass balls on Dirk's bedposts. "This is perfect," he said.

"For what?" Dirk coughed.

"For a tobacco stash," said Pup, depositing another cigarette inside the ball.

After he met Pup, Dirk's room became full of

secrets. The cigarettes in the bedposts. The stolen Three Musketeers bars in the dresser drawer. The *Playboy* magazines under the bed. And the real secret that had always been there grew larger and larger each day until Dirk thought it would burst out licking its lips and rolling its eyeballs and telling everyone that Dirk McDonald wasn't normal.

Dirk looked at the *Playboys* that Pup brought, trying to feel something. All he could think of was that the giant breasts must keep the women safe somehow, protected. As if the breasts were padding for their hearts. His own was so close to the surface of his chest. He was afraid Pup might be able to see it beating there.

Dirk's heart sent sparks and flares through his veins like a fast wheel on cement when he was with Pup. They rode their bikes and skateboards, popping wheelies, doing jumps and flips. Dirk wanted to do wilder and wilder things. It wasn't so much that he was competing with Pup or showing off for him; he wanted to give the tricks to Pup like offerings. He wanted to say, neither of us has to be afraid of anything anymore. Their knees and elbows were always speckled with blood and gritty dirt from falling but Fifi treated them with gel from Love's leaves.

Every morning Pup came by on his skateboard or his bike. He never let Dirk meet him at his house. Dirk wondered what Pup's room was like, what his mother was like.

"You wouldn't want to know," Pup said. "She's just all sad and scared."

Dirk didn't push Pup. It didn't matter anyway where Pup came from as long as they were together. At school they met for lunch. Dirk always had two sandwiches—sometimes he even had peanut butter and jam on waffles, which was Pup's favorite. Dirk rolled his eyes and acted as if Fifi had always given him two sandwiches. He and Pup didn't talk much at school, just sat eating and scowling into the sun. Sometimes girls walked by giggling in their pastel T-shirts, matching tight jeans and pale suede platform Corkees sandals. Pup winked at them, and they tossed their winged hair, smacked their lip-glossed lips. Dirk was glad the girls were too shy to do much more than that. Even the tough boys never approached Dirk and Pup although Dirk was always braced for it, a tension in his shoulders that never went away. It seemed Pup was braced too. His muscles were a man's already, as if his fear had formed them that way to make up for his small size. So the tough boys never bothered them. Together they were invincible. You couldn't find anything nasty to say. They were brown all year long, lean and strong, good at sports, smart; they smoked cigarettes and skateboarded. They wore Vans and their Levi's were always ripped at the knees. The most popular girls dreamed about them.

They shot baskets in strangers' driveways and swam in neighbors' pools and picked flowers and fruits from gardens for Fifi. Sometimes they borrowed dogs from backyards and took them on walks for a while, bringing them home before their owners returned.

It was not just Kaboodle—Pup loved all dogs and all dogs loved Pup. They came running up to him with worshipping eyes and licked his fingers, immediately flopping onto their backs like hot dogs to let him pet their bellies. He always had scraps of bread in his pockets for them.

"What do you think dogs dream about?" Pup asked Dirk one day as Kaboodle lay stretched on top of his Vans, long eyelashes curling as if he had styled them that way.

"I've never really thought about it."

"I think dogs dream about wind and light and leaves and squirrels and birds and when they cry they are dreaming about wolves and freeways. I wish I dreamed about those things."

"What do you dream about?"

"I don't know," Pup said.

Dirk was glad that Pup didn't ask him what he dreamed.

Dirk dreamed about Pup.

He dreamed they were the superheroes Slam and Jam—skateboarding in the sky over the city, rescuing hurt children and animals. The clouds were the shape and color of giant flowers. In Dirk's dream, he and Pup held each other in the center of a purple orchid cloud.

In the summer Dirk and Pup took the bus to the beach with Pup's two surfboards. Dirk never asked where he had gotten the boards but he thought Pup might have stolen them on one of his runs through the neighbors' backyards. As they waxed the boards with Mr. Zogg's Sex Wax to make them glide through the water, Pup told Dirk that surfing wasn't much different from skateboarding.

"You'll be a pro." He looked out at the horizon, measuring the swells.

Dirk followed Pup into the water with the board under his arm. All around him the ocean was blindingly bright, the color of water on a map. Through the sparkles of wet light Dirk saw Pup's smile before Pup paddled out on the surfboard, climbed onto it and was carried away like a part of the wave. Thinking about giving Pup his surfing like an embrace, Dirk plunged into the water with the board, steadying his body as the waves filled and fell beneath and around him.

Afterward they raced up the hot sand and collapsed belly-first onto their towels. They lay there until their hair was dry and the sun and salt water made their skin feel taut against their bones. Then they used the outdoor showers, peeling their trunks away from their bodies, feeling the granules of scratchy sand rinse off from between their legs in the cold water. Pup wrapped his towel around his waist and pulled off his trunks from underneath. Dirk tried not to look. He wrapped his towel the same way and tried to get out of his trunks as smoothly as possible while Pup pulled up his jeans under the towel.

Sometimes after they'd been surfing they sat at The Figtree Cafe on the Venice boardwalk drinking smoothies, eating blueberry muffins and watching the parade. There were velvet and tie-dye women who read tarot cards. Dirk never even wanted them to look at him, afraid they would guess his secret. There were kids break dancing and bulky bronze bodybuilders, a carnival of half-naked roller women, bicycle magician trickster boys, a clown who painted faces, a mocha-colored, electric blue-eyed man in a white turban who played electric guitar and warbled electric songs like a skating genie. There was an accordion-playing devil with a circus cart drawn by mangy stuffed animals on bicycles. More animals dangled from a miniature carousel, and there was a real stuffed taxidermy dog, rigid and nightmarish. Sometimes, to get away from all of it—especially that dog carcass—Dirk and Pup walked under the arcade of pastel Corinthian columns decaying in the salt air, past the vine-covered wood-frame houses and rose-jasmine gardens on the canals and the ducks flapping their feet through the streets like little surfers.

One day after they'd been surfing Dirk started to get on the bus but Pup put his sun-warmed hand on Dirk's surf-sore biceps.

"I know a faster way."

Pup stuck out his thumb. With the freckles on his nose and his bare feet he reminded Dirk of Huckleberry Finn, his Huckleberry friend. Fifi had told Dirk never to hitchhike but Dirk didn't want to be afraid of anything, and besides Pup looked so cute standing there with his thumb out, so defiant and twinkly holding his surfboard, one hip a little higher than the other, behind him the sky turning as pink as the skin on his shoulders where his tan was peeling.

Two girls in a white convertible Mustang stopped. Dirk recognized them—it was Tracey Stace and Nancy Nance, two of the most popular girls from their school.

"Don't you know it's dangerous to pick up hitch-hikers?" Pup teased.

"You guys aren't dangerous. You're too cute," Tracey Stace said. "Besides, you go to Fairfax."

She had dimples and her hair was almost white in the sun, her breasts straining her crocheted bikini top. She was wearing cutoffs ripped the whole way up the sides to show her sleek tan thighs. Nancy Nance was a smaller, less dimpled, less cleavaged version of Tracey Stace. She flopped over into the backseat, and Dirk sat next to her. Pup sat in front with Tracey Stace.

"Want to come over?" she asked. "My mom's out of town."

Tracey Stace lived in a modern house in the hills, all wood and glass. There was a Jacuzzi in the back-yard. She told Pup and Dirk to test the water while she and Nancy got what she called "refreshments." Pup slipped in. Dirk followed him, feeling big and awkward. The blasts of hot water massaged deep into the muscles of his lower back. Tracey and Nancy came out in their bikinis, carrying cold beers and a joint. Their bodies hardly made a ripple as they slid into the Jacuzzi. The moon was full, reflecting the whole of the sun. Lit up with it, the flowers in the garden looked like aliens with glowing skins. The palm trees shook in the Santa Ana winds like the hips of Hawaiian hula girls. Dirk thought about how Fifi called them palmistrees. She said she wondered if you could read their fortunes from above in the sky. He was glad that no one here could read his fortune.

Dirk watched how Pup held the joint and sucked in, narrowing his eyes. He did it too. The smoke burned sweetly in his throat and chest, releasing the place in his shoulders that was always tight, ready to react, to fight back, if someone found out his secret.

Tracey smacked some pink bubblegum-scented gloss from a fat stick onto her lips and moved closer to Pup. Then Dirk watched Pup lean over, just like that, not even thinking, not even trying, and kiss Tracey Stace's mouth. Seeing Pup like that, kissing the most beautiful girl in school, made Dirk want to weep—not just because it was Tracey Stace and not Dirk who Pup was kissing but because of the beauty of it, the way Pup's hand looked against Tracey Stace's back and the way his eyes closed, the long lashes clumping together, the moonlight washing over everything like the waves that Dirk still felt pulling his

body and seething beneath him although they were
now miles and hours away.

Dirk turned to Nancy Nance, who looked very
delicate, like a little girl. He was afraid he might
crush her. Her lashes were like flickers of moonlight
on her cheek.

"You're so pretty," Dirk said. He wanted her to
know that if something went wrong it wasn't because
of that. She smiled shyly at him and he reached out
for her, eyes closed, pressing his lips against hers.

Nancy did all the work after that. Dirk's beauty
was all he had to give her although he would have
given her more if he could. When he felt as if she
would guess his secret he looked over at Pup and
Tracey Stace. Pup had his legs around her and their
bodies were moving up and down in the water.

Then Pup looked at Dirk. When Dirk saw what was
in Pup's eyes his heart contracted with tiny pulses, the
way Nancy Nance's body was trembling near his. Dirk
knew then that Pup loved him too. But mixed with
Pup's love was fear and soon it was just fear sucking
the love away. Pup closed his eyes and there wasn't
even fear anymore. There was just a beautiful boy

with pointed ears kissing a girl in a Jacuzzi, a boy who hardly knew that Dirk existed.

After what had happened with Tracey Stace and Nancy Nance, Dirk knew that everything had changed. Before Dirk and Pup had kissed the girls they were still safe in their innocence, little Peter Pans never growing old, never having to explain. Now Dirk's love for Pup raged through him bitterly. It burned his shoulders like the sun, blistering as if it could peel off layers of skin. It stung like shards of glass embedded in a wound. It jolted him awake like an electric shock.

Tracey Stace and Nancy Nance picked Pup and Dirk up at Fifi's cottage. The girls were wearing tight white jeans that laced up front and back and lace-up T-shirts.

"Where we going?" Pup asked, kissing Tracey Stace's cheek.

"A dance club in the valley," Tracey said.

"We don't dance," Pup said. "We hate disco."

"It's not a disco place. They play KROQ music."

"We still don't dance," said Pup.

Dirk was glad he hadn't told them about dancing with Fifi in the kitchen.

"You can watch us," Tracey said and Nancy giggled.

Dirk and Pup sat behind the dj booth watching Tracey's and Nancy's blond hair change colors under the strobe lights as they danced to Adam and the Ants, Devo, and the Go-Gos. Pup lit up a cigarette. Dirk waited for Pup to hand it to him but instead Pup held out the pack. Dirk took his own cigarette. It was the first time they hadn't shared.

"I scored a whole pack this time," Pup said, as if he were explaining it.

Dirk looked at Pup, far away behind a cloud of blue smoke, moving farther and farther away. Tracey and Nancy were twisting, snaking, shaking and skanking all over the floor. When "Los Angeles" by X came on they butted heads and collided into each other, working their elbows and knees in all directions.

"Punk rock," Tracey shrilled.

Punk rock, Dirk thought as a boy jumped off the carpeted bench along the mirrored wall and began slamming with invisible demons. With his stiff sunglass-black Mohawk, rows of earrings and black leather boots, the sweat and strength of his body, he made Tracey and Nancy's version look like hopscotch.

Dirk could almost feel Pup's heart slamming inside of him as he watched the boy. Dirk knew, seeing that dancer, alone and proud, tormented and beautiful, that he had found something he wanted to be. The boy reminded Dirk of Wild Animal Park.

When he was little Fifi had taken him on the wild animal safari. You had to keep the windows rolled up so the animals couldn't get in. Dirk wanted to get out of the car and run around with them. They were fierce and wise and easy in their skins. That was what the dancing boy reminded Dirk of.

"That dude has some hell of cool boots," Pup said, flicking ashes.

Tracey and Nancy danced over. "She told you this wasn't a disco," Nancy said.

"I think punk is gross," said Tracey.

When they left the club that night Dirk saw Mohawk and three other boys with short hair and black clothes leaning against a turquoise-blue-and-white '55 Pontiac in the parking lot, smoking.

"My grandmother drives a car like that," Dirk said. "A red-and-white one."

He looked back at the boys as Tracey Stace drove away.

"Want to come over?" Tracey asked.

"I'm feeling kind of burnt," Dirk said. "You can just drop me off."

Pup didn't come by Dirk's house the next day. Dirk felt like his stomach was a roller coaster as he rode his skateboard to school. At lunchtime he looked for Pup. He was sitting with Tracey Stace and Nancy Nance.

"What's up?" Dirk asked.

"Not much," Pup said. "You should have hung with us last night. We drove up to Mulholland."

"Where were you this morning?" Dirk asked.

He saw Pup's upper lip curl slightly. "Tracey gave me a ride. We were out all night."

For three days Pup didn't come by Dirk's house. When Dirk finally called and asked him what he was doing that night Pup said, "I'm seeing Tracey." That was all. He didn't ask Dirk to join them.

Dirk saw Pup and Tracey walking on campus with their hands in the back pockets of each other's jeans and knew that he had to do something. If he didn't tell Pup his feelings he thought he might go slamming through space, careening into everything until there was nothing left of him but bruises wilting on bone. He caught up with Pup in the hall after school.

"Are you free today, man?" Dirk asked.

Pup looked like a startled animal caught in the beam of headlights in the middle of a road.

"I'm seeing Tracey," he said. It didn't sound mean, just sad, Dirk thought.

"Just meet me at the tree this afternoon." Dirk walked away.

He didn't really expect Pup to be at the tree where they had first met. It was a warm day but he kept his Wayfarer sunglasses on, kept his sweatshirt on. He practiced skateboard tricks on the sidewalk under the olive tree where Pup and he had put their footprints once when the cement was wet. He was skateboarding over the black stains of smashed olives and the footprints when he heard the thud of rubber

Vans soles on cement, and there was Pup with leaves in his hair just like the first day.

"Hey," Pup said.

"Hey," said Dirk, flipping his skateboard into the air and catching it. He gestured with his head and started walking. Pup walked much more slowly than usual. Dirk could smell his scent—clean like salt water and honeysuckle and grass.

"Want to stop by the house?" Dirk asked.

Pup shrugged. They were silent the whole way to the cottage.

Jimi Hendrix on the stereo. Pup slouched on the floor in Dirk's room while Dirk unscrewed the bed-post and took out what he had hidden there. He shook the pot into the paper and rolled and licked the way the boy who had sold it to him had done. Then he lit the joint and handed it to Pup. Pup took a deep hit and handed it back. Dirk breathed in smoke like the green and golden afternoon light. Maybe it would make him brave.

"Nancy really likes you," Pup said after his second hit. "She's a babe."

"She is," said Dirk.

"You should've gone with us up to Mulholland."

Dirk wanted a magical plant to grow inside of him, making him proud and at ease. He and Pup smoked some more. Jimi's guitar burned with music.

"I just wanted to tell you. I've been pretending my whole life. I'm so sick of it. You're my best friend." Dirk looked down, feeling the heat in his face.

"Don't even say it, Dirk," said Pup.

Dirk started to reach out his hand but drew it back. He started to open his mouth to explain but Pup whispered, "Please don't. I can't handle it, man."

He got up and pushed his hair out of his eyes. "I love you, Dirk," Pup said. "But I can't handle it."

And then before Dirk knew it, Pup was gone.

That night Dirk stood in the bathroom looking at his reflection. He didn't see the fine angles of his cheekbones, the delicate bridge of his nose, the tenderness of his lips. He didn't see the sparkle of his dark eyes that seemed to shine up from the deepest, brightest place. He saw a scared boy who was in love with Pup Lambert and who hated himself.

Dirk took a razor and began to shave the sides of his scalp. The buzz vibrated into his brain. How thin was the skin at his temples, Dirk thought. Just skin stretched over pulse. He thought about the punk rock boy at the dance club. There was something about that boy that no one could touch. Dirk took the hair that was left on his head and dyed it with black dye so that it was almost blue. Then he formed it into a spikey fan. He smoothed it with Fifi's gel and sprayed it with her Aqua Net so it stood straight up like the hair on top of Kaboodle's head.

At school Dirk wore all black and his Mohawk. Everyone turned and stared. But no one had questions in their eyes about what it was all hiding underneath. The disguise worked. There was some fear, some admiration, some jealousy, but no one despised Dirk the way he knew they would if he revealed his secret.

Also, no one questioned why Dirk and Pup didn't share a lunch on the same bench anymore, why they didn't play basketball together. It all seemed because of the Mohawk, the big boots Dirk had started to wear, the Germs and X buttons on his collar. That seemed like enough. No one knew that it was because of a glance in a Jacuzzi, a joint shared like a kiss and then turned to ash, a shock of love.

Dirk and the
Tear Jerks

Fifi watched Dirk and his Mohawk more closely now. Her blue eyes looked always ready to spill. Dirk wanted to tell her, how he wanted to tell her, but what if the tears spilled, blue onto her cheeks? What if he hurt the one person who had loved him his whole life? What if she said, "It's just a phase," and he had to tell her, "It's not just a phase, Grandma Fifi. It's who I am."

And why did he have to tell? Boys who loved girls didn't have to sit their mothers down and say, "Mom, I love girls. I want to sleep with them." It would be too embarrassing. Just because what he felt was different, did it have to be discussed?

On Dirk's sixteenth birthday Fifi called him into the kitchen.

"Where's Pup?" Fifi asked. "I thought you were going to invite him over."

"He's busy," Dirk said. "You know that. You ask me every day."

Kit came and sat on Dirk's lap. Kaboodle covered his eyes with his paws. Pet and Mini did a tragic ballet in their cage.

Fifi had baked Dirk a chocolate raspberry kiwi cake. The candles made her shine like the Christmas tree angel she put on her pink-flocked tree each year. Dirk closed his eyes and blew the candles out. He didn't make a wish. There were no wishes inside of him anymore.

"I have something for you, sweetie," Fifi said.

Kaboodle winked at him and licked frosting off his fingers.

Dirk followed Fifi outside, Kaboodle bouncing at their feet so that his tongue swung with each step. Fifi's red-and-white 1955 Pontiac convertible was parked in the driveway. It had a huge red ribbon tied around its middle.

"I know it's nothing you haven't seen before," Fifi said. "I would have gotten you a new car if I could have."

"You're giving me your car!"

He stroked the cherry red, the vanilla white, the silver chrome. It was like a sundae, like a valentine, like a little train, a magic carpet.

"Well, if you want it. Now that you can drive I thought it would be a good present. It's very safe. They made those things sturdy back then. And I'm getting a little too old to drive."

"I'll be your chauffeur. I love it, Grandma," Dirk said.

Then he noticed something different about the car. Mounted on the front was a golden thing.

"What's that?"

"It's a family heirloom. A lamp. It comes off the car, but for now I thought it looked splendid as a hood ornament."

"What's it for?"

"When you are ready you can tell your story into it," Fifi said. "You can talk about Pup—whatever you want to say. Secrets. Things you can't tell anyone."

"I don't have anything to say."

"Someday you may. Someday it might help."

Dirk looked at the golden thing. He was afraid of

it. He wanted Fifi to take it back. But what could he do? Anyway, he had the car and that's what mattered. With the car he didn't need Pup; he didn't need anybody. He could drive through the canyons with the top down, race along Mulholland's precarious curves, looking at the city glistering below. He could feel the breeze kissing his naked temples, more tender than any lover. Go to punk gigs by himself. Slam in the pit with the boys until the pain sweated out of him, let the pain-sweat dry up and evaporate in the night air as he drove and drove.

But Dirk didn't go out that night. Instead he lay alone in the darkness. His hands kept wandering over his body wanting to touch himself the way someone would rub a magic lamp in a fairy tale to make a genie appear. But Dirk pulled his hands away. He wanted to cut them off. He wanted to turn off his mind. He tried to think about Nancy Nance but all he could see was Pup Lambert.

Dirk remembered what Fifi had said to him. How could he tell his story, he wondered? He had no story. And if he did no one would want to hear it. He would be laughed at, maybe attacked. So it was better to have no story at all. It was better to be dead inside.

He looked up at the billboard models looming above like hard angels in denim as he drove down the Sunset Strip one night. I would rather have no story at all, Dirk decided. I want to be blank like a model on a billboard. I want to be untouchable and beautiful and completely dead inside. But he thought of the stuffed dog he and Pup had seen on the Venice boardwalk, so long ago it seemed now—a rigor mortis display. Without a story of love would he become only that?

Dirk was going to see X at the Whiskey A-Go-Go. He had a fake ID he had made himself using his new driver's license. He had a black leather motorcycle jacket covered with zippers that he had found at a musty dusty cobwebs-and-lace thrift store for only ten dollars. He had his warrior Mohawk. Kaboodle was sitting next to him on the front seat with gel in his shock of hair and his big paw resting on Dirk's leg.

The dark club was full of pierced, painted boys with shaved heads. They were slamming in the pit in front of the stage, throwing their bodies against each other in a wild-thing rumpus. Dirk felt that he fit in here much better than at school. Exene wove around

with her two-tone hair hanging over her eyes and her
arms and legs sticking out of her little black dress
like the limbs of a doll that had been thrown around
too much. John Doe's face looked even whiter against
his black hair as he twisted it into expressions of tor-
ture and ecstasy, baring his teeth or pouting like
James Dean. Billy Zoom's platinum ice devil smile
never left his lips as he played his guitar at crotch
level. The music made Dirk think of black roses on
fire. He wanted to leap onstage and dive into the crowd
the way some of the boys were doing. He wanted to
play music that would make the boys in the pit sweat
like that. Maybe that was how those boys cried, Dirk
thought. Maybe he would start a band called the Tear
Jerks. For a moment he remembered sitting in his
room with Pup, Pup holding the guitar, but he let the
drums beat the thought away. His own band. Dirk and
the Tear Jerks. Tear Jerk Dirk.

His throat and heart felt tight, constricted with
dryness, so he bought a beer and gulped it down.
Then he went and stood at the edge of the slammers.
Some boys behind him were moving up and down in
place, jostling him forward. Finally he flung himself

into the writhing body mass. It was like surfing in a way, fighting to stay up above seething waters that wanted to consume you, part of you wanting to be consumed, to vanish into radiance.

"The world's a mess it's in my kiss," X sang.

Dirk felt the bitterness and anguish making his lips tingle. He raged arms and legs akimbo into the fury. He was carried forward by the whirlpools of the crowd to the stage. On the stage. Blinded sweat tears lights. Howling. Panic. Pandemonium. Pan, hooved horned god. Flinging himself off into space. Waiting for the fall, the hard smack, unconsciousness.

No. Buoyed up. Thrilling sweat-slick biceps. Cradled for a moment. Father. Father. Objects in flight around the room. Fragments of poetry. Lost eyes far away. Eyes like boats drifting farther and farther away.

He was back on his feet again. The crowd had caught him. He had felt their respect and admiration. He wiped off sweat with the back of his hand and went to get another beer. As he walked through the crowd he felt some bodies move back to give him room, witness his strength, others brush against him to feel it. The lights caught zipper metal and raven hair. Sweat on tan skin like beer drops brown glass glisten.

After the show Dirk gave Kaboodle some water and walked him until he peed. A boy and girl with matching burgundy hair that stood straight up on their heads like flames smiled at them.

"Mohawk dog," the boy said. "You're twins." Dirk and Kaboodle smiled back.

They got in the car and drove by Oki Dogs on Santa Monica Boulevard. Punks, kids with long greasy hair and junky-bulky veins in shriveled arms, tall men with big cars and sharp teeth, sat on the scarred benches under fluorescent lights that buzzed like flies or fat cooking. Dirk stopped the Pontiac and got out. The man at the counter shouted at him, "Okay okay," so he just said, "Oki Dog and a Coke." The Oki Dog was a giant hot dog smothered with cheese and beans and pastrami slices and wrapped in a tortilla. Dirk ate a few bites. It tasted salty greasy rich dark danger like the night. He was so hungry.

Then he saw a shrink-wrap swastika earring. It was dangling from the ear of a girl with spikey hair. The girl was drinking a Coke and giggling with her friends. She could have been Tracey or Nancy with a punk haircut.

"Do you know what that earring means?" Dirk said. He had never spoken out like this but suddenly his nerves felt huge, fluorescent, explosive. Maybe from the music still in his head. Maybe from the symbol.

The girl giggled. "It's a punk thing."

"Do you know who Hitler was?" Dirk asked.

"Yeah sure."

"Really? You know about the concentration camps?"

"Kind of. I guess. Why?"

"Hitler massacred innocent people. I'm sure you heard about it sometime. That was his symbol. The swastika."

"I got it at Poseur. It's cool."

"It is so uncool. You can't even believe how uncool it is," Dirk said.

The girl lowered her eyes. She looked to her friends and back to Dirk.

Dirk left Oki Dogs and got in his car. Kaboodle kissed his face and Dirk gave him the rest of the Oki Dog. As they drove away Dirk saw the girl pull the earring out of her ear and look at it.

So maybe it wasn't what he thought, this scene. But it was a wild enough animal safari that his own beastliness might go unnoticed.

He drove over the city's shoulders tattooed with wandering, hungry children and used car lots, drove past hanging traffic light earrings into beery breath mist, up and up above the city, trying to shed it like a skin. On the city's shaved head was the crown of the Griffith Observatory. The viewing balcony was closed, but the star Dirk had come to see was the bronze bust of James Dean on its pedestal. He gazed into its light and would have exchanged his soul for that boy's if he could.

Because he couldn't give his soul to James Dean, Dirk kept going out. Just keep going out, he told himself.

The Vex was a club in an old ballroom. Dirk drove into the parking lot under a freeway, concrete shaking like an earthquake. Inside there was a long curved bar and columns and balconies and chandeliers but everything looked ready to crumble from age and the

freeway vibrations. Dirk watched a boy and girl slamming. The boy threw the girl down on the ground. She
was wearing a lot of metal that shocked against the
wood of the floor. He started hitting her in the face.
Finally some guys broke it up but to Dirk it seemed
like it went on forever. There was blood the color of
her lipstick on the girl's face.

Dirk felt the piece of pizza he had eaten for dinner hot in his throat and ran into the bathroom. When
he looked up under the greenish-white chill of the
lights, his head felt as if he had slammed it against
porcelain.

After that, Dirk drove along Sunset to the
Carney's hot dog train.

"Do you have a dollar?" The boy sitting in front of
Carney's looked like Sid Vicious. "I'm Sinbad," he said.

He was really skinny so Dirk motioned for him to
follow him in. But when they were sitting on the
bench outside, Sinbad said he didn't want the hot dog
Dirk had bought.

"I'm a vampire," he said.

"A what?"

"A vampire."

He bared his teeth. He had fangs.

"They're bonded on," he said. "They really work. Want to see?"

"No," Dirk said.

"Don't you want to exchange blood with me?" He leaned closer on the bench.

"Get away from me," said Dirk.

"You don't know what might happen," said Sinbad.

Two boys walked by, leaning against each other, sharing a frozen yogurt.

"If you ask me all those fags are going to die out," said Sinbad.

As he got in his car, wishing he had brought Kaboodle for a kiss and a wink, Dirk thought of Sinbad's eyes. They were familiar. Where had he seen them? Then Dirk knew he had seen those eyes in the mirror when he scrutinized his face for blemishes and imperfections, when he imagined that no one would ever love him.

Fifi was volunteering at a local hospital the next night. Dirk was home listening to his Adolescents album.

"I hate them all—creatures."

The angry voice made Fifi's collection of plaster Jesus statues shake as if there were an earthquake, or as if they were about to start slamming, Dirk thought. He imagined a pit full of slamming plaster Jesuses. He didn't like the thought.

Suddenly Fifi's music box with the ballerina on top began to play, the ballerina going around and around on one toe. The china cabinet doors flew open and Fifi's coaster collection spun out like tiny Frisbees. Dirk covered his head to protect himself. The clown paintings on the walls swung back and forth, and Dirk thought he heard them laughing evil clown laughter. Dirk had never liked the clowns. He turned away from their leering mouths and saw the plaster Jesus statues slamming. Dirk stared into the eyes of one of them. The eyes were glowing. The statue fell from the shelf and its head broke off but the eyes kept sizzling like fried eggs. Finally the Adolescents' song was over and the house was quiet. Dirk heard an owl hooting in a branch outside the window and some cats screaming. He could have screamed like that. He plucked his wet T-shirt

away from his sweating body and collapsed on the
bed.

Fear, the band, was playing out in the valley. Dirk
armed himself in chains and the leather motorcycle
jacket. He rode the 101. The freeway made him think
of loss instead of hope, stretching out under a hovering orangish buzz of night air, not seeming to lead
anywhere. At night the valley felt deserted. Dirk
drove down barren streets under tall streetlamps. The
little houses looked blank, as if they wanted to deny
that anything unpleasant happened in or around
them, but the way they were nestling under the crackling telephone wires, Dirk knew they were afraid.

Dirk got to the place where Fear was. Punks were
hanging out in the parking lot drinking beers, smoking, grimacing—everything out of the sides of their
mouths. White-bleached hair bright under the blue
lights, black-dyed hair stiff with hair spray, ears and
noses pierced with metal, backs covered with leather.
Some boys were giving each other tattoos with ink and
needles. One boy was burning his arm with a cigarette
butt while a girl shrieked at him. Dirk couldn't tell if

she was laughing or crying.

He went inside. The lead singer's square white head and hate-filled mouth seemed blown up, larger than life. As the music speeded, Dirk climbed out of the pit, up onstage and flung himself into the slamming mash of bodies. As he fell into the sweating arms he felt desire inside and around him but it was a brutal thing, feverish and dangerous. He looked into the eyes of one boy and saw that the desire was mixed with a hate so deep it had the same shape as the swastika tattoo on the side of the boy's vein-corded neck. Dirk knew there was nothing he could say to the boy that would change what he thought about the thing inked so deep into his flesh, inked so deep into him. It wasn't like shrink wrap. But he said it anyway.

"Fuck fascist skinhead shit."

Swastika and two other boys with the same tattoo followed Dirk outside when the show was over.

"Where you going, faggot?" the first boy said.

Dirk felt they had looked inside of him to his most terrible secret and it shocked him so much that he lost all the quiet strength he had been trying to build for as long as he could remember.

"Fuck you," he whispered.

The skinheads were on him all at once. Dirk saw their eyes glittering like mica chips with the reflection of his own self-loathing. He wondered if he deserved this because he wanted to touch and kiss a boy. The sound of everything was so loud and he kept seeing the skinhead skulls with the stubble, the bunches of flesh at the back of the neck like a bulldog's. His own head felt like a shell. A thin one you could crush on the beach. He had never realized how delicate his head was. This pain was hardly different from what he had always felt inside—torn, jarred, pummeled. In a way it was a relief—a confirmation of that other pain. But he wanted to escape it all finally.

He wanted to die.

When the blood had stopped pouring enough for him to see, Dirk drove home. He never knew, later, how he made it. He had to stop every so often to lean his head against the wheel. Blood was all over the car upholstery.

Once when he looked up from the steering wheel he saw a house crossing the road. It was a cheerful-looking yellow house moving on wheels through the valley night. Dirk thought at first he must be hallucinating. Then he thought, my father. He didn't know why but that was what he thought. He leaned his head back down and when he looked up the house was gone.

When he got home finally he managed somehow to get the lamp Fifi had given him off the front of the car and carry it inside. He staggered to the bathroom and washed the gashes on his face while Kaboodle whimpered at his feet and gently pawed his leg. His reflection pitched and blurred in the mirror. Blood was caking now, turning darker and thicker.

Dirk steadied himself by leaning against the wall until he got to his bed. He fell down there and closed his eyes.

Dirk dreamed of the train. It was moving through the hills, through the forests like a thought through his mind, like blood through a vein in him. There were the fathers taking their showers. They were naked and close together under the water. But something was different. Thin fathers. Emaciated bodies. Shaved scalps. Something was happening. What was happening? Not water. Gas. Coming through the pipes. Gas to make their lungs explode. Dying fathers as the train kept going kept going kept going. To hell.

part two

Gazelle's Story

Kit was lying over Dirk's heart staring at him, her usually aloe-vera-green eyes now black with pupil. Even Kit could not take away the pain flashing and shrieking through Dirk's body like an ambulance. His blood shivered.

Help me; tell me a story, Dirk thought, knowing that somewhere in the room the lamp was waiting. Tell me a story that will make me want to live, because right now I don't want to live. Help me.

He shut his eyes.

The wind was tapping the peach tree's long thin leaf fingers against the window. The moon cast shadows of the branches across the floor. Dirk sat up in bed and Kit jumped off of him, yowling. It felt as if Dirk's heart leaped out of his body with her. In the corner of the room beside the golden lamp the figure of a woman was seated on a chair. She was wearing a long dress of creamy satin covered with satin roses and beads that shone like crystals under rushing water, raindrops in the moonlight. There was a veil over her face but Dirk could see her pallor, the sadness in her eyes. Eyes like his own. He clutched his wild-duck-printed flannel pajama shirt closer around his chest impulsively but he was no longer cold. And the pain was far away now—a fading red light, a retreating siren.

Am I alive? Dirk wondered.

He wished that the woman would go away. But she looked so sad; she looked as though she needed to talk to him.

"Who are you?" Dirk said softly into the darkness.

"My name is Gazelle Sunday. You want me to go."

"No I don't."

Was she about to cry? Dirk didn't want her to. He tried to think of something.

"Do you have a story?" Dirk asked.

"A story?"

"Yeah. I don't have one."

"I can't remember," she said.

"I bet you can. I bet you are full of stories. I can see in your eyes."

"No, no, not really."

"Try to think." He really wanted her to tell him something now. "Maybe something about that dress. Where did you get that dress?"

The woman reached her almost-transparent hand out to him.

"Please," he said.

"If you will dance with me."

"Okay," said Dirk, and then wondered if that was such a good idea. She looked like death. He wondered if she would dance away with him. Dance him to his grave. Maybe that was the best thing. Maybe that was what he wanted. Or it had happened already. And besides he had promised, and she, this white ghost lady, had begun to tell.

"I never knew my mother but I knew she had given me my name and I loved her for that. I imagined that my mother and father were from France, very young, very in love. In my mind they looked like children in the book of fairy tales—the only thing besides my name that my mother had left me. The book was big and full of intricate, jewel-colored pictures of castles with turrets, enchanted mossy forests, goblins, banshees, trolls, brownies, pixies, fairies with huge butterfly wings and djinns on magic carpets. I pretended that the two children in one story were my parents. I saw them walking into the woods, their faces as pale as the snow they trudged through, their eyes big dark mirrors like the frozen lakes they had to cross, their mouths like petals ripped from the red roses that they waited for all winter but never saw again, dying in each other's arms when I was born. At least that is the story I told myself, walking in circles, twisting my hair around one finger, sucking my lower lip, holding the book open in my arms.

"I lived with my aunt in a dark and musty building. The kitchen smelled of boiled cabbage and potatoes; the claw-foot bathtub behind the screen in the kitchen corner smelled of mildew no matter how hard I scrubbed it clean. I was always leaning my head out the window to smell the bay, the baking bread, to hear the trolley car ringing its bell as it crested the steep hill. In the parlor was a dressmaker's mannequin. I was afraid that if I misbehaved the mannequin would attack me with the needles and scissors my aunt used to make dresses.

"My aunt was a cold woman with raw hands and a mouth that looked as if it was always full of pins. She hated me. I knew that the only reason she let me live with her at all was because I helped her sew. I became a better and better seamstress. I could do the most elaborate embroidery and beadwork with my tiny fingers. I could make roses out of silk; they looked so real you hallucinated their fragrance. Women came from all over the city for my dresses. My aunt never let me wear what I made. I had one black frock and a brown one for Sunday church—the only day she let me out of the house. I didn't mind the hard work, really, or the plain clothes or even the fact that I couldn't leave and had no friends. But I wanted to dance. I needed it. Dancing was the only thing I wanted. I would do it in secret. With a child's wisdom I knew never to let my aunt see. She thought it was a sin."

That's like me, Dirk thought. Like me loving boys,

not wanting anyone to know.

"When she went out I pulled back the carpets. It was very strange. Whenever she went out some beautiful music would start to play in the apartment next door. I learned later that it was Chopin. It was like a magical being from my fairy book had entered my body when I heard the music. I felt the strong center of who I was pulsing with the sound of those fingers on the piano keys; it radiated out through my limbs until I became like a giant butterfly or a silk rose, a waterfall, fire. I never saw anyone come out of the next-door apartment but it didn't matter—the gift of their music made me feel I had finally found a friend. I danced wildly the story of my parents, of my birth, my life with my aunt. I saw worlds beyond the parlor as if I were soaring through the air on a magic carpet, cities twinkling like fairies or the crowns of giants, and forests green and singing with elves."

In just the way that Gazelle had seen those cities and forests, Dirk saw, there before him, a Victorian parlor and a slim girl dancing among coffinlike furniture draped in dark shawls. She had a child's body in old-fashioned white underwear but her eyes and mouth were a woman's. She was spinning as if she wanted to make herself dizzy, falling to the floor where she twisted and turned and tangled in her pale hair, each motion full of longing. Dirk heard, too, the faint strains of piano music ghosting the air.

"I danced till I was nauseous and sweating through my underthings," Gazelle went on. "I had to change before my aunt came home. I knew she was coming because the music always stopped in time for me to change and get back to work. But one day even when the music stopped I kept dancing. I couldn't stop. I heard the music inside of me still. So that when my aunt came into the room I didn't even look up. I was kneeling on the floor, running my hands all over my body. Then I opened my eyes and I realized there hadn't been music for quite a while. My aunt was looking at me with scissors in her eyes.

"She grabbed my arm and pulled me to my feet.

"'What were you doing?' she said as if she were snipping pieces out of the air.

"I told her I was dancing.

"'Do you know what happens to girls like you?' my aunt said.

"I saw the mannequin in the corner. The cloth I had covered it with had slipped off. I imagined that the mannequin had needles sticking out of her body and was ready to shoot them across the room at me.

"'Girls who touch themselves grow up ugly,' my aunt said, like a curse. 'No one will ever marry you. No one will want you because you will be a little monster. You are the devil's bride. He plays music in your head.'

"And it was worse than being whipped. It was as if she had broken my legs with that. I never heard the music again. I never danced. I never told my story.

"When I bled for the first time a few months later my aunt saw the stains on my underthings and said, 'You see. You see what happens to girls who touch themselves. They bleed like little monsters. But they don't die. You will wish you died, I think, because you will always be alone.'"

"Oh my God," Dirk said. "How could she do that to you? She was sick."

Gazelle wrung her hands. She was trembling.

"Are you cold?" Dirk asked her. He took a blanket off the bed and held it out.

"Oh, no thank you. How kind you are. Kind, like him."

"Who?" Dirk asked.

Gazelle's eyes filled with tears. "He saved me, finally. I thought I was a monster. I huddled and hunched in my black dress. My fingers cramped like an old woman's. My face grew twisted with pain. There were always bruise-blue circles under my eyes from holding my tears back. Without my dancing I was like the mannequin in the corner, no arms or legs, swaddled and bound. I never left the apartment.

"But he came to me finally. It was my sixteenth birthday, and my aunt was out. It wa   windy evening full of spirits. I almost thought I heard my piano player through the walls but it was only the wind. There was a knock on the door."

As she spoke, Dirk saw the parlor again, the image quivering as if behind smoke or water. The girl was older this time, and her body looked as if it had never danced and never would. Dirk gasped to see how different she was, almost as ravaged as the woman in white. He wished he could have waltzed her out of that place.

She hobbled over to a door and opened it. There stood a small man with dark skin and blue eyes. His head was shaved so that his sharp cheekbones seemed to stick out even more.

"I shivered with awe when I saw him. I felt my whole life lived in that moment—blooming from a seed in my mother's belly, swimming like a tiny slippery fish, growing a birdlike skeleton, clawing forth—a baby lynx, dancing as a girl, becoming a woman with a child inside of me, lying in a satin-lined coffin beneath the earth while a young woman danced the story of her life above me.

"'I need you to make a dress for my beloved,' said the man in a voice like a purr.

"'Come in,' I said.

"He sat on the brown sofa. I noticed a red jewel embedded in his nose. It caught the light like a tiny fire.

"'I want you to make me the most beautiful dress,' he went on. He reached into the sack he was carrying—he must have had a sack of some kind although I don't really remember it now. But how else could he have brought the fabric in? I remember the fabric. It was a bolt of thick cream Florentine satin. And he also gave me the most fragile lace—all chrysanthemums and peonies and lilies and baby's breath—and a golden box full of tiny crystal beads.

"He put all these things in front of me.

"'I'll need to see the woman in order to make it,' I said. I imagined a fairy woman with dark skin and pale eyes like his, jewels in her ears and nose and on her fingers, chunks of rubies, emeralds and sapphires like her eyes. I would have been afraid to touch a woman like that—to have her there at my fingertips, just on the other side of the satin, vulnerable to my pins and needles. But I wanted to see her, too.

"'I want the dress to be a surprise for her' was all he would say.

"'Do you have her dress size and measurements?' I asked. I was very shy. I kept my head down the whole time I spoke to him. But I had to look up to see his answer because he was silent, just shaking his head and looking at me.

"'Well, how will I know what size to make it?'

"His eyes on me were like the softest touch, a touch I had not known since the last time I let my own hands caress my now monstrous, bleeding body, since the last time I danced. They were the color of blue ball-gown taffeta.

"'Looking at you . . . I think she is just your size,' he said.

"I blushed so much that I thought I was the color of the ruby in his nose. How could he know about my body beneath the black shawl I wore bundled around me? But I agreed to make the dress.

"Then he left. I almost danced again. I did dance in a way—my fingers danced over the satin. I sat at the black-and-gold sphinx sewing machine and made a ballet of a dress—the most beautiful dress. When I was finished he came back. My aunt was away. He asked me to put the dress on.

"I went into the back bedroom, so dim and draped in dark fabrics to keep out the light, and I put on the dress. The satin against my skin made me want to weep. The dress felt cool and warm, light and soft, supple and strong the way I imagined a lover would feel. I looked at myself in the stained mirror and hardly recognized the gleaming woman, skin as pure and pale as the satin, eyes lit with the candleshine of the dress, lips moist with the pleasure of the dress, who stared back at me.

"I came out into the parlor and showed the stranger. He sat forward on the sofa and looked at me with a hypnotic blue gaze.

"'Thank you,' he said. I started to leave the room to change but he called me back. He put a large stack of bills on the table and rose to leave.

"'Wait,' I said. 'Don't you want it? Isn't it right?'

"'It is perfect.'

My eyes were full of questions.

"'The dress is for you, Gazelle. And there is something else I want to give you.'"

Dirk watched Gazelle take the golden lamp to her breast as if it were a nursing child. "I asked him what it was," she said.

"What did he say?" Dirk whispered.

"That it was the place to keep my secrets, the story of my love. But I told him I have no story."

Like me and Fifi, Dirk thought.

"He said, 'Yes you do. We all do. Someday you will know it.' He started to leave then, and I brushed my fingers against his shoulder. His eyes looked into

mine—big pale sky crystals full of sorrow and wisdom. Lakes full of first stars that I wanted to leap into,
wishing.

"'Please,' I said.

"He took my hands in his. His hands weren't
much bigger than mine but they were powerful and
hot, the color of the cocoa velvet I used to sew winter
hats. He put his lips to mine. I felt the room fill up
with satiny light and a sweet powdery fragrance.

"'You must not be afraid' were the last words he
said to me.

"The next month I didn't bleed. At first I thought
that my aunt's curse was over—I wasn't a monster
anymore, I had been good. But when my belly got
bigger and bigger I thought that her curse had
become even more powerful.

"'Oh, I knew you were evil,' she said. 'It must be
the devil's child. Who else could have touched you?
Who else would have touched you?'

"I thought about the stranger. Could he have been
the devil? If he was the devil I would have gone with
him anyway. I wished he would come back."

"How could she say those things to you?" Dirk

asked. "What happened? Did you have your baby?"

"Yes. She told me we would put it up for adoption when it was born. And she locked me in my room so the women who came over for fittings wouldn't see me. She only opened the door to give me food and the material to sew. I wanted to die. I might have killed myself with the sewing shears except for three things—the baby inside of me, the magical dress hidden in mothballs and tissue in my closet and the words I heard purring through my head. 'You must not be afraid.'

"Then just before my baby was born my aunt fell ill. She let me out of my room, and I sat at her bedside pressing damp lavender-soaked rags to her forehead and feeding her soft food."

"You should have strangled her," Dirk said. "Sorry. But I think she deserved it."

"She was a damaged woman. I would have been too if the stranger hadn't come. Someone had seen her touch herself, maybe even seen her dance, and told her those horrible lies."

Dirk said, "You're kinder than I am," and she answered, "No, not really. I was just trying to protect my baby, you know. I remembered all the fairy tales about the evil witch cursing the child. She'd almost destroyed me, and I wasn't going to let her hurt the baby."

"Did she?"

"No. She died rather peacefully with my hands on her temples. Poor thing, I think I might have been the first one to touch her in all those years."

"Then what happened?"

"I gave birth to the most beautiful little girl! The most perfect little girl. She had tiny naturally turned-out feet and fluttering pink hands like wings and she danced everywhere. From the moment she came out of me she was dancing."

Dirk saw the phantom parlor again, although this time the walls were freshly painted white; the floral friezes along the ceiling were pale pink and blue. Lace curtains like bridal veils hung at the open windows. He thought he heard the piano music again.

"I painted the inside of the house and kept the windows open all day," Gazelle said. "I sewed large floral tapestry cloth pillows, pink, blue and gold, and stuffed them with dried lavender and rose petals. I recovered the brown sofa in jade-green velvet. I made a chiffon canopy over the bed and lit long tapers so that through the draperies the house looked full of stars. I built fires in the fireplace that my aunt never used, and the house smelled of cedar smoke. I read poetry aloud—Shelley and Keats. 'The silver lamp—the ravishment—the wonder. The darkness—loneliness—the fearful thunder,' only it was a golden lamp and there was no more darkness.

"My daughter, who loved to draw, made a picture of a lovely face and put it on the mannequin under a big hat covered with birds' nests full of pale blue eggs.

"'Now you won't be afraid of her anymore,' she said, child-wise.

"No longer prisoners, we went out into the city that had been forbidden to me for so long. We walked up and down the hills until our legs ached, then rode the trolley car to feel rushes of salty, misty air. We had picnics and fed the swans on the lake under the flowering terra-cotta arches, drank tea and ate pastries in rooms with cupids and rosebuds painted on the walls, strolled through the park, green-dazzled, fragrance-drunk, gasped at treasures gleaming gold in the half-lit glass cases of the museum. Then we'd return with spices, fruits and vegetables from Chinatown, seafood and baguettes from the wharf.

"The piano music began again—coming through the walls every evening—and I watched my child dance. It was almost as if I were dancing myself. She danced among the spools of thread, the ribbons and laces, the silk flowers.

"After a while I took her for ballet lessons from Madame Joy. I brought her to the studio four times a week. She was the littlest in class but the very best; everyone thought so. I made her a garland of silk blossoms and some tiny pink net wings. She always played sprites or pixies in the dance recitals. I sat and watched her with such pride.

"Sometimes, though, she wouldn't stick to the choreography. She couldn't help it, she'd just start doing her own dances. Madame Joy hated that.

"'What are you doing, idiot-child!' she screamed.

"She took her cane and hooked it around my baby's waist; she hit it against her backside. I was mortified when I found bruises on her.

"'I don't want you going back there,' I said. 'You can dance at home.'

"But I knew she missed performing. I sat and watched her for hours, shining a light on her, but it wasn't the same.

"One day when we were walking down the street she started to jump up and down, tugging my fingers and pointing. Two little boys in spangled blue costumes were taking turns balancing on each other's shoulders in front of a crowd. She let go of my hand and before I could stop her she had jumped into the act, climbing up the tree of the boys to pose on top like a Christmas angel. They made her spin like a music box ballerina. The crowd cheered. I was so proud. After that Fifi joined the act."

"Fifi!" Dirk said.

"Yes. Your grandmother."

"I didn't know all this about her childhood," Dirk said. "Or about you." He was embarrassed that he hadn't even heard Gazelle's name before.

"That's because you never asked."

Dirk knew that was true. He had just assumed that Fifi was always a spun-sugar-haired grandmother living in the cottage, alone.

"And she never asked about my life," Gazelle

said. "And I never asked about my aunt's. That's the way children are sometimes. Until it's too late. If I had asked my aunt about herself it might have helped her. It's important to tell your story. It's important to listen."

"Tell me more," Dirk said.

"The years went by. Fifi danced with Martin and Merlin, first on the street and then in cafés. Everyone thought that either Martin or Merlin was her beau so Fifi never had any gentleman callers. Sometimes I would find her crying into the tulle and silk of her dancing costume.

"'What's wrong?' I would ask her. 'Your dress will be so heavy with tears the boys won't be able to lift you.'

"'No man will like me,' she said. 'I'm such a cricket, an insect.'

"'Don't say those things,' I scolded. I was afraid that somehow I had passed on to her the self-hatred my aunt had given me, although I was always telling her what a great beauty she was and that her size only added to it. Still, she did her stretches diligently, hoping they would make her taller. She wore the highest heels she could find, although I warned her about her feet, and did exercises to increase her bustline.

"I told her that I thought people believed she was engaged to Martin or Merlin, that she might not encourage that so much, but she wouldn't hear of it. She always held their arms when they walked down the street and let them introduce her as their fiancée sometimes. It was her way of protecting them, you see. In those days their feelings for each other weren't something people talked about. Of course, it was quite obvious to me. When they performed they would hand her back and forth between them like a love letter."

"Like a love letter," Dirk said.

"Yes. They loved each other."

"I know," said Dirk. "What do you think about that?"

"Any love that is love is right," Gazelle said. "It's the same as me touching myself when I was a child. Do you understand?"

"Yes," Dirk said. "I understand." Something in his body opened like a love letter. He wondered if Fifi would understand about him. . . . Maybe she had all along.

Gazelle went on.

"Fifi always played along with being engaged to Martin or Merlin, depending on whose relatives were at the show. But it enforced the feeling that no man would love her the way she dreamed of being loved. She became more shy, staying home all day drawing and painting in the parlor. Sometimes we went to the countryside where she set up an easel and painted the fields full of cows, the wildflowers and redwoods. She loved color. She used to say how she would paint everything if she could, eat orange or green porridge, cover the ceiling with flowers, make her hair pink or purple."

"Fifi the original punk," Dirk said. "She just needed a man as wild as she was."

"Well, she found him. One night she was performing at a supper club. As she left the theater in her gold brocade coat, peach roses in her hair, she was stopped by a tall, dark, sad-eyed man. He tipped his hat to her and a hundred fireflies came swarming out, surrounding her and lighting her up as if she were still on stage."

"'How did you learn that?' she gasped.

"'I'm an entomologist,' he said. "But magic like

this only happens when you meet your true love. My name is Derwood McDonald.'"

"McDonald," Dirk said. "My grandfather. He was a bug guy?"

"That's right," said Gazelle. "I wouldn't call him a bug guy. He was a magician really."

"That's what the bug ambulances are about, I guess," Dirk said. "When Grandma Fifi finds an insect in the house she gets an old yogurt container or something and makes this siren noise. She puts the bug into it and takes it outside. She calls it a bug ambulance."

"That's my daughter," Gazelle said. "Anyway, just then her partners appeared and took her arms.

"Derwood McDonald introduced himself to them and added, 'I was going to ask you to dinner, Fifi, but you look as if you already have plans.'

"She told him she didn't have plans, that she saw Martin and Merlin every day and every night.

"'It's true,' they agreed, nodding in unison. From all their performances they had become accustomed to moving as one.

"'Fifi might enjoy some new company.' They

bowed and walked off, side by side.

"By the time Fifi and Derwood got to the restaurant there were so many ladybugs on Derwood's jacket collar that they looked like red polka dots.

"'You must have very good luck,' she said.

"'I am having it now,' he answered.

"They ate pasta and drank red wine. She told him about her dancing, how she loved to draw and had started to take art classes.

"'I won't always be able to do those adagio tricks,' she said. 'I'm trying to plan for my future.'

"He told her, 'You will probably dance when you are ninety years old. You remind me of the fairies I saw in the countryside when I was a boy. My father—he was a naturalist too—pointed them out to me as if they were just another form of insect so I never understood why people thought they were made up. They had wings like large honeysuckle blossoms and were finger-size, but otherwise you look just like one. After I grew up I thought I'd never see another fairy,' he said. 'Until I laid eyes on you. Are you a fairy, Fifi?'

"Fifi giggled. Derwood laughed too but his fairy-filled eyes remained sad.

"He walked her home. She came into the house flushed and happier than I had ever seen her. I thought of the night the stranger had come to my door.

"'What is it, Fifi?' I asked.

"She knew even then that she loved him, that she wanted to marry him."

"On Sundays Derwood took Fifi to the countryside. They caught butterflies in a net, studied the beautiful paintings of their wings and set them free. When Derwood found dead butterflies he would take them home and make collages that he framed behind glass. He and Fifi looked for fairies too, but never found any."

"'It doesn't matter,' Derwood said as she came back with dirt on her hands and leaves in her hair from searching through grottos and barrows. 'You are my fairy.'

"In the evenings Derwood came calling with honey from his bees. It tasted like nothing less than nectar made for the love of a golden queen by a hundred droning drones. We slathered it on homemade bread, drizzled it over rice pudding, let big shining drops fall into our teacups and blended it into sauces for the salmon we ate on Fridays. I played the phonograph and Fifi danced. Sometimes Martin and Merlin came over too and they all performed for us. Derwood sat on the jade-green sofa among the rose- and lavender-stuffed pillows wringing his hands during the most precarious balances, clapping and stomping when a trick had been executed."

"But as much as Fifi loved Derwood I could tell something was wrong.

"Finally, after Fifi had known him for a few months and he still hadn't kissed her, she asked him what it was.

"'I have a heart condition,' he told her. 'The doctors tell me I only have a few more years to live.'

"Fifi wanted to run away from him.

"Derwood said, 'I will understand if you don't want to see me anymore.'

"Fifi broke into tears but her sobs sounded like the flicker of crickets. Hundreds of ladybugs flew and landed on her hat. Cocoons opened and butterflies were released in a storm. She held on to Derwood in the forest of wings, and a golden powder covered their faces. Fifi was afraid they would be suffocated, but the butterflies only seemed to be kissing their cheeks.

"'I want to be with you, Derwood McDonald,' Fifi said. 'No matter what.'

"A golden ring slid down out of the air and moved across the picnic cloth toward Fifi. She gasped when she saw the two tiny ring bearers.

"'These are my pet spiders, Charlotte and Webster,' Derwood said. 'They want to know if you will marry me.'

"Not wanting to waste a moment, Fifi and Derwood were married the next day. Fifi wore the dress I had made for the stranger. Hundreds of pink doves flew alongside Derwood's car on the way home.

"Derwood and Fifi lived in a gingerbread house a few blocks away from me. It had two tall columns in front and cherubs bearing garlands over the windows. It was painted lavender but it was like a greenhouse full of flowering plants, butterflies, crickets, doves. Thin sheets of tin, pressed with the patterns of rib-boned urns full of cascading leaves, covered the walls. Derwood studied his insects by the light of the Tiffany lamp. Fifi, who was still taking art classes, drew the insects Derwood loved, and made them dance—balletic butterflies, tangoing tarantulas, waltzing caterpillars and tap-dancing bees.

"Fifi and Derwood hated to be separated, even for moments. Wherever they went they held hands. At night Fifi danced for him, swirling around in her glittery dresses, bringing tears of joy to Derwood's eyes.

"'I knew you were a fairy,' he said.

"Fifi peeked at him from behind a lavender ostrich-feather fan.

"'Then I can make all your dreams come true.'

"He took her in his arms and kissed her as the pink doves watched from the rafters and ladybugs and spiders and butterflies sang silently along with the radio. Fifi knew, though, that she and Derwood had only one dream and that she could not make it come true. It would take a much more powerful fairy than Fifi to cure what was wrong with Derwood's heart.

"At night she put her head on his lean chest and heard it ticking like an explosive. Fifi did make many of her dear Derwood's dreams come true before he died.

"'You make my dreams come true every night,' he whispered into her wispy hair as they fell asleep, fearless from the wine of love.

"And one night, Fifi knew that she was pregnant.

"'I'm pregnant,' she almost shouted.

"'You mean just this second?'

"'Yes.'

"'How do you know?'

"'I know. I'm a dancer. I've always known things about my body.'

"Derwood put his hand on her flat stomach. Her narrow waist and hips didn't look big enough to hold a baby. Fifi listened for Derwood's tears in the darkness. Instead she heard the soft, damp crackle of his smile.

"So she had made another of his dreams come true. His son, Dirby McDonald, your father.

"Dirby was born a very serious little boy. His father was afraid to get too close to him because he knew their time together would be so short. Fifi was so busy worrying about Derwood that she didn't give the child the attention he needed. I tried to care for him but he was always far away in his own world. He was a mystery to me.

"Finally one day, while Fifi and Derwood were out on one of their excursions to the countryside,

Derwood sat down by the bank of a shallow, shimmering creek. A giant white butterfly flew past, and Fifi ran after it. She wanted to show it to Derwood. Maybe, she thought, the butterfly is really the fairy we have been looking for. But she couldn't catch it. When she got back to the creek Derwood was lying on his back. His face was covered with butterflies. They seemed to be trying to get inside of him or maybe they were coming out of him. But Derwood did not struggle. By the time Fifi had run to his side the butterflies were scattered and Derwood was dead. Fifi drove Derwood's car back to the house and collapsed on the front step before I had time to open the door with Dirby in my arms. There was Fifi lying in a heap. For a moment I didn't recognize her. Her hair was completely white. Dirby didn't cry. He just stared like an old man who has seen many deaths, his face tight and drawn. I put his white-haired mother to bed. She wouldn't eat for days. She seemed to be shrinking.

"'I never really believed he would die. I don't want to live without him,' she said.

"'You have to live, for Dirby and me,' I said, holding up her son for her to see. Oh, your father looked like you, young Dirk. He looked like his own father too.

"It made Fifi weep to see Derwood's eyes in that young face but she reached out for him, and when she did the doves in the rafters sang again, and the peonies in the arboretum unfolded layers and layers like Renaissance ruffs.

"'You see,' I said, 'you must hold on.'

"Her art school teacher sent her work to an animation department in Hollywood. They wanted to hire her.

"'I don't want to leave you, Mama,' she said. 'I stayed alive so I could be with you and Dirby.'

"I told her she had to go. 'There are groves of orange trees—you can pick your breakfast every morning—fountains in the hillsides, starlets in silk stockings driving colorful jalopies with leopards in the passenger seats, sunshine all the time. The sun will be good for Dirby. He's as pale as his old grandmother.'

"'You should come with us,' Fifi said, but I couldn't. I was afraid to travel and besides, what if my stranger returned and I was gone?

"So they prepared to leave, Fifi and Dirby with Martin and Merlin in a big old automobile with the glitter-and-paint dance backdrops of swans and heavens and circuses and fairylands fastened to the top.

"I gave Fifi the stranger's lamp as a good-bye gift. I still didn't believe I had a story to tell. A self-imposed shroud of silence had covered me long before the real shroud of death made it impossible for me to speak. But my daughter would have a story, I thought; Fifi would fill the lamp.

"She didn't want to take it from me but I made her promise. Just before she was to leave, the story that I still did not believe was mine came to an end.

"And now it's time for you to dance with me," Gazelle said softly.

Dirk stood up slowly, aware of how light he felt, and held out his arms. She was like Fifi's feather boa—not only that weightless but she brushed his skin with ticklish flicks of softness. She smelled like his grandma too—cookies baking, roses, almonds. Gently, gently Dirk and his Great-Grandmother Gazelle danced around the room while the peach tree tapped at the window and the moon made a shadow forest on the floor. Dirk saw the story of her life repeated now with the sway of the white dress, the pleatings and swishings of satin.

"Thank you, Dirk," Gazelle said, when the dance was over. "Bless you. You listened. You listened."

Death came for me, Dirk thought. She was fading away as she had come and he thought he would dissolve with her, molecules shifting without substance into veil of spirit.

Be-Bop Bo-Peep

And that was when the guitar in the corner began to play by itself.

Dirk opened his eyes. The guitar seemed to be floating on its side, strings trembling with music. Strands of smoke were flying out of the golden lamp and whirling around the guitar.

"Daddy," Dirk said out loud, remembering something he had lost a long time ago.

And Dirk's daddy Dirby McDonald's face appeared out of the smoke just above the guitar, as handsome as James Dean, not much older than Dirk, eyes soft with love like a lullaby behind his black-framed glasses. Lullaby eyes.

"Dirk," his father said, "hang on now."

Dirk nodded. He could taste blood in his mouth

like he'd been sucking on a dirty metal harmonica.

"You came back," Dirk said.

"You want a story. A wake-up story. A come-back story."

"Yes. Please," Dirk said. "Please tell me who you are. I've always wanted to know. I feel like I don't exist. I feel like I'm spinning through space losing atoms, becoming invisible, disintegrating. I . . ."

"Shhh, now," Dirk's father said. His voice was gentle. It was like his guitar. Like his eyes. Dirk thought, His eyes are guitars.

"What do you want to know?"

"What you felt. Who you were. Why you died."

"I always felt lonely," Dirby said. "It was just who I was born to be. I felt more like a part of nature than like a boy. Do you know what I mean?"

Dirk wasn't sure.

"I'd look at the stars in the sky or at trees and I'd want to be that. I worried Fifi. She was always trying to get me to be normal—play with the other kids, laugh more. She took me to her bungalow on the studio lot and showed me how she made the limbs of creatures move by drawing them again and again on clear sheets with light shining through. One of her projects was a story about herself and my father. The fireflies had devilish grins, the ladybugs had long eyelashes, the honeybees sang like Cab Calloway and the spiders danced like Fred and Ginger. She tried to get me to laugh, but I just asked questions about how butterflies hatched from cocoons and how spiders made their webs. I wanted to walk in the hills at night and get as close to the moon and stars as I could. I wanted to lie in the dark grasses of the canyon and listen to the wind play them like the strings of a guitar. I wrote poetry from the time I could write. That was the only way I could begin to express who I was but the poems didn't make sense to my teachers. They didn't rhyme. They were about the wind sounds, the planets' motion, never about who I was or how I felt. I didn't think I felt anything. I was this mind more than a body or a heart. My mind photographing the stars, hearing the wind. My forehead was lined before I was sixteen and I was always thin no matter how much Fifi tried to feed me."

Dirk looked at his father's body in the black turtleneck and jeans. Dirby's frame was just like

Dirk's with the broad shoulders, narrow hips and long legs, but Dirk weighed at least fifteen pounds more and was lean himself.

"When my father died and I saw my mother's hair turn suddenly white I decided I was going to be like the clouds passing over the moon or the waves sliding up and back or the birds putting sounds together. That was the only way I could go on, accepting the way life was, being in the world.

"Then one night when I was sixteen I hitchhiked down into Topanga Canyon. I loved it there—the wild of it so near the sea, the thickness of trees and the smell of salt water all sharp and clean. I had to get away from the sugar smell in Fifi's kitchen and the roses; as much as I loved her I felt like I couldn't breathe—like it wasn't my world in any way.

"I walked inside this canyon bar and for the first time in my life I felt at home with walls around me. There was a cat onstage playing saxophone and chicks in black stockings sitting around watching him. There was beer and smoke—not just cigarettes, the kind of smoke that helps ease you into trees and wind. I knew I'd be coming back here.

"I came back all the time—every chance I could get away. All I needed was my thumb and my poetry journal. I also got a black turtleneck from my father's closet and a black beret from a thrift store so I'd look like the other cats hanging there in the mystic smoke and swinging sax night.

"One night a skinny old guy wearing shades asked me what I was writing in that journal all the time and I told him poetry.

"'You're a baby. What do you know about poetry?' he said, all languid-like.

"'I know enough,' I said.

"'Yeah. I bet you know some nursery rhymes. Little Bo-Peep come blow your horn the cat's in the meadow the chick's in the corn. That's poetry, right?'

"I tried to walk away from him but he called after me, 'That's poetry, right, Bo-Peep?'"

"After that everyone called me Bo-Peep. Until the night I got up on that stage, sat down on a stool in the moon of light and read what I'd been writing all those nights.

"Everyone got still, especially that old man. They leaned in close to dig the words. But it was more than words. Something was happening. There was this bottle of red wine and four glasses on the table next to me and they started dancing, I mean really dancing, doing some kind of tango-fandango number. Then the shades on the face of the old man jumped right off and started floating in the air, moving just out of his reach when he grabbed for them. I saw his eyes with the pinpoint pupils and red whites and knew why he wore those shades but there was nothing I could do about what was going on. I just kept reading. They were all digging it more and more, even the old guy. More stuff kept going on. My beret flew off my head and went slinging across the room onto the head of this beautiful chick. She had short hair like a boy's, almond-shaped eyes and breasts that were the shape of one of those stiff padded bras but I could tell, even from the stage, that she wasn't wearing one. She was wearing a black dress and black fishnet stockings on the longest legs I'd ever seen. She laughed and put her hands to her head where my beret had landed. Her girlfriend handed her a joint but it didn't stay between her long fingers. It flew right out of those fingers and across the room, landing in my hand. I swear this is all true, buddy. Not that it sounds like the truth but it was."

Dirk was less stunned by the thought of his father's words making wineglasses dance than by what he saw hovering behind Dirby. When he saw her he remembered the way her long eyelashes had felt, ticklish as butterflies against his skin, he remembered the smoke of her voice and the patchouli smell in her hair, her long glamorous legs in black stockings. She was more beautiful than any girl in a magazine, she the boyish goddess. She was Edie Sedgwick and Twiggy and Bowie and like his father she was James Dean too. Just Silver. Mother. While Dirby kept talking she did a slow rhythmic dance, hands over her head, torso moving with sinuous snakey charm.

"Mom," Dirk said.

"After, I stopped reading my poetry, things settled down," Dirby went on. "I mean no more dancing wineglasses or flying joints, but everyone went wild.

"The old guy came up onstage—he had his shades again—and said, 'This, my friends, is Be-Bop Bo-Peep, beat guru.'

"I wanted to get out of there fast but the beautiful

chick reached for my arm when I passed her table and put the beret back on my head. She smelled like incense and patchouli and orange blossoms. The light caught the big silver hoops she wore in her ears.

"'I dug that, Be-Bop,' she said.

"I just nodded the way I'd seen the hipsters do when someone dug them.

"'My name is Just Silver,' she said. 'Just Silver with a capital J capital S. The Just is because I renounced my father's name.'

"'Are you a model?' I asked.

"She was. An actress too. She had done little theater and had a tiny part in a Fellini film once.

"'You are very, very beautiful,' I told her. I knew I sounded more like Bo-Peep than Be-Bop talking like that but I felt she had dug right into my heart.

"She asked if I'd read *Siddhartha*. It was my favorite book. She told me I reminded her of him.

"'Come home with me,' she said.

"She drove me in her black convertible VW Bug to her apartment above the Sunset Strip. There was no furniture in the apartment—just rugs. Just Silver's family had traveled all over India and the Mideast purchasing rugs when she was a child. She lit some Nag Champa incense—flowers turned to powdery stick stems, turned to clouds of smoke petals—put on some Ravi Shankar and made her head move from side to side on her neck like an Indian goddess. Then she cooked vegetable curry with rare saffron that was the color of poppy pollen.

"'Do you know what this is?' she asked, showing me a dancing metal goddess holding a severed head and wearing a necklace made of skulls.

"'I might think twice about getting into her car if I was hitching,' I said.

"'Would you really? I don't believe you.'

"'You're right. I'd get right in. She is beautiful.'

"'She's Kali, the blessing, dancing goddess. She's also death. In the East those things can go together.'

"I knew what she meant. She danced for me for a while and then we lay on her mattress and made love all night.

"After that I didn't feel any less lonely, only that Just Silver had joined me in the wild blue windscape of my loneliness.

"'I'm pregnant,' she said one night as I felt her draw me inside of her like a mouth on a pipe full of a burning dream-plant.

"'What? Just this second?'

"'Yes.'

"'How do you know?'

"'I am very in touch with my body.'

"'I can tell.'

"'What are we going to do?' She said we, knowing somehow that I wasn't going to leave even though I reminded her of Siddhartha.

"'I never had a dad,' I said.

"'I'm sorry. What happened?'

"'Well I had him for a while but he died when I was five. He knew he was going to die so even when he was alive he kind of ignored me.'

"Just Silver kissed the angles of my face. Her hair smelled like Nag Champa and marijuana. Her eyelashes were so long they looked like they hurt her. Her legs were as long as mine when we lay hip to hip and measured. Steep thighs.

"'So you don't want a baby,' Just Silver said. 'I mean, because of your dad.'

"'No. I want a baby because of my dad. I want a baby so I can be a dad for him.'

"'Or her,' Just Silver said.

"'I think we will have a boy.'

"'Why?'

"'I'm very in touch with our bodies.'

"'I can tell.'

"So we decided to have you, buddy. We almost named you Siddhartha but Fifi convinced us it was not going to be fun for a little boy to grow up with a name like Siddhartha, and Sid didn't have the right feeling. Fifi liked the name Dirk because of the sound of Derwood and Dirby and so we agreed, although your mother didn't see much difference between Dirk and Sid.

"Fifi loved your mom as if she were her very own daughter. She was so happy to see me with a friend. I had really never had any friends. Now Just Silver and I went everywhere together. I would recite my poetry and she would do her interpretive dancing on the stage. The wineglasses danced with her. I had expected things to stop moving around when I fell in love but I was just as telekinetic as ever. Maybe more so.

Instead of grounding me, my love sent me spinning even deeper into the center of loneliness that was the stars and the night and the wind. I didn't feel that my love was anything to do with the planet I had been born on. I wanted to fly away with Just Silver.

"Then you were born. You presented me with this problem. How was I supposed to keep living this abstract way, trying to be like music from a horn, like sweat, like the dark skin of night peeling back at dawn? Although I'd wanted a baby so I could love it the way my father hadn't been able to love me, when I saw you with your eyelashes and toes and every-thing, I realized what a big responsibility you really were. I had to care in a way I had never had to care before. I read you poetry and played my guitar. I made your toys fly around the room like planets in space. But I was drawn more and more to the waves and the wind. You made my heart hurt too much. It ached so much I thought it would stop pumping like my father's had.

"Your mother and I would leave you with your grandmother and go driving for hours. We liked to take Sunset all the way to the sea. We kissed in the furious Santa Anas that felt like jewel dust whirling around us as the sun went down.

"The night we gave up on life, I can't say it was a conscious decision. But we didn't struggle against it either. That was the year Martin Luther King and Robert Kennedy were killed. In a way I think it was all too much for us—this world."

Dirk thought of his parents on the precipice, wanting to sink into the cavern of night and wild coyote hills, away from the hammering headlines and screaming TVs and the death of fathers.

"That's why I want you to be different, Dirk," said Dirby. "I want you to fight. I love you, buddy. I want you not to be afraid."

"But I'm gay," Dirk said. "Dad, I'm gay."

"I know you are, buddy," Dirby said. And his lullaby eyes sang with love. "Do you know about the Greek gods, probably Walt Whitman—first beat father, Oscar Wilde, Ginsberg, even, maybe, your number one hero? You can't be afraid."

"Maybe it's too late," Dirk said. "Dad, am I alive now?"

"Yes. Still. Fight, Dirk."

"Mom?"

And then his mother, still dancing behind Dirby, all eyelashes and legs, spoke with that dream-plant smoke voice, "Tell us your story, Baby Be-Bop."

Genie

"Ｏne night when he was little Dirk McDonald woke to the sound of the telephone and his Grandma Fifi's voice," Dirk began.

"He had never heard a voice sound like that. Dirk looked up at the glow-in-the-dark stars Grandma Fifi had pasted on the ceiling for Dirk's father when he was a little boy. She had told Dirk they would keep nightmares away. But that night Dirk thought nothing would ever keep him safe from nightmares.

"Grandma Fifi ran into the bedroom and took Dirk in her arms. Her bones felt as light as the birdcage that hung in her kitchen. She wrapped Dirk in a coat that smelled sour from mothballs and lilac-sweet from her perfume.

"Dirk sat huddled next to his grandmother in her

red-and-white 1955 Pontiac convertible and felt as if the night was going to eat him alive; he wished it would. Fifi hadn't taken time to put the top back on. She ran through red lights. Dirk had never seen her do that before.

"When they got to the hospital a doctor met them in the hallway and led them back into the waiting room. Fifi took Dirk on her lap. Dirk could never remember, later, if the doctor had ever said the words, but he knew then that his parents were gone. He pressed his face into the velvet collar of Fifi's coat and their tears mingled together until they were drenched with salt water.

"Dirk listened for his parents' voices in the wind sometimes. But soon he forgot what they had sounded like. All he could hear was his Grandma Fifi whistling with her canaries in the kitchen or calling to him to come out and play in the yard or asking the pastry dough what shape it intended on taking this afternoon or singing him lullabies."

Dirk went on to tell the story of life in Fifi's cottage, the fathers in the shower, the story of Pup Lambert and the magic lamp. He told the story of Gazelle and the stranger, Fifi and Derwood, Dirby and Just Silver. All his ancestors' stories were also his own.

Each of us has a family tree full of stories inside of us, Dirk thought. Each of us has a story blossoming out of us.

"Dad?" he asked the darkness. "Mom?" but Dirby and Just Silver were gone.

He picked up the golden lamp. It was heavy with stories of love. It was light with stories of love. It could sink to the bottom of the sea, touch the core of the earth with the weight of love. It could soar into the clouds like a creature with wings.

Just then he saw that the lamp had begun to smoke—vapors writhing out from it like snakes. And Dirk saw emerging from that mist the face and then the whole body of a man. There was a piece of sapphire silk with golden elephants on it wrapped turban-style around his head. Dirk knew that beneath the turban, the man's scalp was shaved; he was the stranger who had come to Gazelle's door with the very lamp out of which he was now materializing.

"Come with me," the man said.

"Where?"

"You'll see."

The braid rug on the floor of Dirk's room began to quiver. Then the corners furled off the wooden floor and the rug lifted from the ground, bringing with it Dirk in his bed. Dirk closed his eyes the way you do on a roller coaster, wind and gravity forcing lids down, forcing him to grip the brass posts as the bed levitated. Eyes still closed but he knew he was outside now careening through star-flecked space on warm wind, part of him wanting to scream, wake from the dream, part of him letting this be, this journey to wherever, this journey on the voice of the man.

Beneath him the city the way it looked from inside the Japanese restaurant on the hill where waitresses in flowered silk kimonos brought starbursts and blossoms of sushi maki and champagne in silver ice buckets. A platter of gleaming wineglasses and luminous liqueurs, main courses served on polished plates, towering flaming desserts, candlelit birthday cakes. And on to the edges where it was darker and on to the sea that broke against the shore in seaweed black against iced jade pale. Dark waves becoming pale foam like the banks of wild dill and evening primrose growing along the highway. Ancient stone creatures emerging from the sea. Fields full of cattle. Some were there to die. He saw a bull mount a cow like a wave of life in the midst of static death. Fields full of farmworkers, sweat stories hidden behind the clustering clean sea green, sea purple of the grapes they picked. Redwood groves purple shadows light fallen like pollen through high leaves. Sea going so far it looks like sky. Just blues forever. Sky like a field of lupine and white wildflower fluffs. Sheer rivulets of water a skin of light over the sand. On and on. Where was he going?

In a field at the edge of the sea was a white house with crystals and lace in the window. Trumpet vines grew over the trellis and picket fence in front. A hammock in the garden. On the porch were surfboards, sandals, sleeping golden retrievers.

Duck Drake and his family lived in the house that smelled of beeswax and lavender and home-baked bread. Duck's mother Darlene had wide-apart green eyes, frothy yellow hair and petite tan legs. She liked to stand on the porch having long conversations with the mockingbird who lived in the garden. She was always asking Duck questions about what his favorite flower was and why and what was his favorite color and time of day and animal and what dreams did he have last night? Duck's brothers and sisters, Peace, Granola, Crystal, Chi, Aura, Tahini and the twins Yin and Yang, were always careening through the house like a litter of blond puppies yelping, "I'm not delirious, I'm in love."

Duck was the only one who never talked about his crushes since his crushes were on boys and Duck knew Darlene wouldn't understand at all. He thought it was strange because of how free she was about other things. Once she tried some pot brownies that Peace made but she said they just made her depressed and unable to stop giggling. She let Crystal's boyfriend sleep over and she had told all the girls that when they were ready to have sex she would take them for birth control. But when it came to Duck's secret he knew she wouldn't accept it. He had heard her talking to her best friend Honey-Marie about Honey-Marie's son Harley. Harley was a few years older than Duck, and Duck had always admired him from afar. He looked like he was born to play Prince Charming with his fistfuls of curly dark hair, flashing dark eyes and ballet dancer's body. He spoke in a soft rich voice and wore baggy cotton trousers with Birkenstocks and colorful socks. Harley was a waiter at a café in Santa Cruz but he really wanted to go to San Francisco and perform Shakespeare. Finally, just before he left, he told Honey-Marie that he was gay. She was devastated. Duck heard her tell his mother, "My heart is broken."

Then he heard his mother say, "It could be worse. He could have something really wrong with him."

He breathed a sigh of relief on the other side of the kitchen door.

"Something *is* wrong with him," Honey-Marie said.

Then Duck's mother said, "I guess you're right. I'd probably feel the same way if it was my own son."

After that Duck tried. He took Cherish Marine to the prom and bought her a huge corsage of pink lilies. He even rented a tux (although he would not put his feet in weasel shoes and wore his Vans instead). Cherish Marine was a bathing suit model and all the boys wanted to be her date but she liked Duck with his lilting surfer slur and teenage-Kewpie beauty. They danced all the slow dances and Duck felt Cherish Marine's bathing-suit-model-breasts pressing through her peach satin prom dress. They went to the pier with a group of other kids and shared a bottle of champagne which Cherish Marine liked to drink with a straw. They sat next to each other on the roller coaster, Cherish Marine's slender thigh pressing against Duck's leg, her hands grabbing his knee as their light bodies were thrown from side to side of the car, bruising, the metal bar hardly enough to keep them from being flung into space. But when the evening was over Duck walked Cherish to her door and kissed her good night on her smooth peachy cheek. She looked into his eyes waiting for something more but he only said, "You are a total babe. Thank you for being my date," and left.

Cherish Marine was stunned.

Duck went surfing because it was the only thing that comforted him. When he surfed he felt as aqua-blue and full and high as the waves but he also felt lost, a small human who could as easily be washed away as his father Eddie had been. Even the other surfers were separate from each other in their own tubes of water. Once in a while he'd see a guy holding his girlfriend and once he had seen a guy surfing with a pig on a leash. Duck wanted a boyfriend he could surf with, someone he could tell his secret to, someone who had the same secret inside. He wanted to reach inside his lover and touch that lonely secret with his own.

Duck decided to leave Santa Cruz. He drove his light-blue VW Bug along Highway 5 listening to the B-52s. He opened the windows and let the wind run its fingers through his shoulder-length hair that was bleached white from years of surfing in sun and salt water.

I am finally free, Duck thought, and then he thought about his brothers and sisters and his mother telling them not to get sand all over everything and please be quiet so I can do my yoga, Duck could you please pick up some tofu patties for dinner, you look just like your daddy I miss him so much he would have been so proud of you the way you rode that wave.

The soaring free feeling was mixed with a sadness as Duck realized how alone he really was now. It was kind of like surfing—but then, Duck thought—everything was kind of like surfing.

Duck got to Zeroes at night and built a fire at the campground. He heated up a can of beans and watched the waves, nodding with encouragement at the good ones like a proud father, watching the sun drop into the sea. He thought of how his father had died in the ocean and how instead of hating the water or being afraid of it he loved it even more. He didn't understand why that had happened to his dad but now he knew that his dad's spirit was there in the waves protecting him. He wondered if his father would understand about how he loved boys. Somehow he thought that if his dad were alive his mom wouldn't have agreed with Honey-Marie. She would have been too happy basking in her love for Eddie Drake. Around Eddie Drake everyone just basked—they felt safe, they didn't judge. Duck had never heard his dad say a negative thing about anyone's personal choice—just about things like the Vietnam War and the assassination of Martin Luther King and what was happening to the oceans. Even now after his death, he was like the sun—falling into the waves, rising again every morning—still with Duck like a god in an ancient myth.

Duck slept on top of a picnic table that night with his arm around his surfboard. He looked up at the stars and wondered if the future love of his life was looking up at them too. He couldn't have known about the glow-in-the-dark stars on the ceiling of a room where a boy lay wishing for Duck.

Duck waxed his board and surfed-in the dawn; he felt as if he was pulling the sun up behind him as he rode the waves. Then he rinsed at the outdoor showers. He wanted to stay out by the water forever but he knew that if he was going to live in Los Angeles he would have to try to get work.

He applied at a surf shop in Santa Monica. He had worked at one in Santa Cruz and he knew a lot about boards. Plus there was something about Duck that made people like him right away—his grin and the innocent openness in his blue bay-window eyes. The owner of the shop told him he could start the next day.

When evening came Duck drove into town—to Santa Monica Boulevard. He had never seen so many gay men all at once. He felt the buzz of desire making them all beautiful. Everything was sexy here—hamburgers and ice cream and books and boots and even supermarkets became sexy. There was even a billboard advertising gay cruises. The men on the billboards were all tan and muscular and the men on the streets looked like they had stepped off the billboards. Music thumped out of bars, and through the doors Duck saw strobe lights pulsing. He wanted to dance. He had never danced with another man. Some men came out of a club with their hands in each other's back pockets. Sweat was pouring down their necks and arms. Someone whistled at Duck. He was afraid to look at who it was.

"Do you have some money for food?" a boy asked him. The boy had huge brown eyes. Duck gave him a couple of dollars even though he hadn't had dinner himself.

"Thanks, man," the boy said. He was different from some of the other guys around there—really young with a sweet mouth. When he smiled Duck saw that he had a gap between his front teeth. On the sidewalk in front of him was a huge chalk drawing of a beautiful blue angel.

"You new around here?" he asked.

Duck shrugged, not wanting to admit that this was his first time. His mouth felt dry and his heart was like the music coming out of the bars. "That's a good drawing," he said to change the subject.

"Thanks. Want to go to Rage?"

"Sure," Duck said.

The boy stood up and wiped his chalky hands on his jeans. Duck followed him into the bar that was crowded with men. A lot of the men knew the boy.

"Hey, Bam-Bam!"

"Is that you?" Duck asked.

The boy cocked his head. "Bam-Bam, yeah. Why?"

Duck started laughing. "My name is Duck," he said.

"Well at least it's not Pebbles."

Bam-Bam was a wild dancer, flinging his arms around and around over his head, gyrating his torso and hips. Duck found out later that sometimes he worked as a go-go boy when he could get a gig. Unfortunately it didn't pay much and most of the time Bam-Bam was out on the streets spare-changing or doing whatever else street kids did for some quick burger bucks.

"Where are you from?" Bam-Bam asked Duck over some beers that a guy in leather chaps had bought for them.

"Santa Cruz."

"And this is your first time out."

"What do you mean?"

"Out. Coming out."

"Oh. Yeah," said Duck. "I mean no."

"It's cool," Bam-Bam said. "Everyone has to have a first time."

"What about you?"

"I'm from all over. I was in Frisco last. I just keep moving. I'm a mover. I'm not from anywhere."

Duck nodded. He figured that wherever Bam-Bam was from—everyone had to come from somewhere, right?—it wasn't a two-story white wood frame house full of crystals and waffles and laughing golden children. Maybe Bam-Bam really did come from nowhere. Duck had noticed some cigarette burn marks on Bam-Bam's bare, thin arms. Parents that did stuff like that to you had to become nothing nowhere in your head if you were going to make it out alive.

Duck and Bam-Bam went to the beach and slept on the picnic tables. In the morning Duck surfed while Bam-Bam sat on the sand and sketched him. Duck made them coffee, boiling water over the campfire.

"Do you like L.A.?" Duck asked.

"It's okay I guess. It'll be better when I get my shit together. I design furniture."

"Like what?"

"Well for now it's just drawings." Bam-Bam opened his sketch pad. He showed Duck pictures of tables made from surfboards and other ones covered with a mosaic of bottle caps and broken glass and china. There was some neo-Flintstone-style furniture made from broken slabs of stone and boulders, and some shaped like dinosaurs.

"You fully rip," Duck said.

Bam-Bam smiled so the gap between his teeth showed.

"So where do you live?" Duck finally asked.

"Sometimes I can find a squat. Sometimes I go to the shelter. When I have money I get a motel with some other kids. Why, you looking for a place?"

"Today I'm going to go look for an apartment," Duck said. "If you want you can stay with me for a while."

"How much?"

"It wouldn't cost you anything. And you could get off the streets."

Bam-Bam looked suspicious. Duck hoped he hadn't hurt his feelings. "I just don't know anybody out here," he added. "You could kind of show me around. You could design me a table. Just don't use my surfboard for a table!"

Duck and Bam-Bam found a one-bedroom apartment on Venice Beach. Duck surfed every morning and worked at the shop all day. At night he took an acting workshop but he was always too shy to present anything. After a while the teacher, Preston Delbert, just gave up and ignored Duck. But Duck kept going, sitting in the back, wondering if he would ever find a voice inside of him or something to say with it.

Bam-Bam stayed home painting murals of the ocean on the walls, designing furniture and making omelettes or peanut butter sandwiches for him and

Duck to eat. He cut Duck's hair short so that it looked like the petals of a sunflower. Duck suggested that maybe Bam-Bam should take a class in furniture design at a city college or go to beauty school but Bam-Bam said he wasn't ready. He stopped going out altogether. He said he was afraid that he'd get caught back up in street life. At night, Duck and Bam-Bam slept in the same bed holding each other but they didn't make love. Bam-Bam said he didn't feel like it and Duck was too shy and inexperienced to push him. Duck wondered if he would ever know what it was like to make love to a boy he loved. Sometimes he wanted to go back to Rage or do something wild in a men's room or cruise in a park but he was afraid. He felt that he had to be responsible too, and set a good example for Bam-Bam.

One day Duck came back from work and saw that Bam-Bam's things were gone. There was a picture of an angel, like the chalk one on the sidewalk, painted above Duck's bed. Under it was written, "I love you, Duck. You will find your true angel. I am a dangerous one. Bam-Bam."

Duck sat on the bed and cried. He wasn't sure

why he was crying so hard. I didn't know him that well, Duck told himself. He was a street kid. He couldn't stay inside with me forever. He wasn't my boyfriend, he didn't even want to make love with me. But still Duck cried. He was crying for the first person who knew his secret and for the painter of angels and for the warmth of those thin, cigarette-burned arms and maybe for something else—a premonition of what would happen later.

After Bam-Bam left, Duck went out every night, prowling the streets, maneuvering through them as if he was surfing perilous waves. He never talked to the men he touched in bathrooms and parks and cars. Is this what it means to be gay? Duck wondered. He missed the clean, quiet beaches of Santa Cruz, the softer sun and the sparkling, swirling colors of the waves and sky, the cathedral forests of redwood trees and the way he saw rabbits or long-legged baby deer who hopped like rabbits and heard the soft motorcycle hum of quail in the woods near his house. He missed being cleansed by the ocean he had practically grown up in, hiking home with his smiling sunlit dogs, sitting in the reeds by the pond listening to the frogs as evening slowly settled. He even missed the skinned-looking yellow slime banana slugs on the forest paths. Mostly, though, Duck missed his mother and his little brothers and sisters. He thought he could hear them squeal, "I'm not delirious, I'm in love!"—the words Duck felt he could never say. I guess I deserve this, Duck thought, holding a man in a cold-tiled, sour-smelling men's room. In the dark he could not even see the man's face and he was glad because he knew the man couldn't see him either.

Where are you? he called silently to his soul mate, the love of his life whose name he did not yet know. By the time I find you I may be so old and messed up you won't even recognize me. Maybe this is what I deserve for wanting to find a man. Looking for you always, never finding you, poisoning myself.

Then the lights from a passing car revealed the eyes of the man whose hands were on Duck. The eyes were like tile. Duck shivered.

"Faggot," the man said. "How much do you hate yourself, faggot? Enough to come to piss stalls in the night? Enough to die?"

Duck tried to wrench away but the man had fingers in his arm like needles. He tried to scream but no sound came out of his throat to echo against the walls of the empty men's room.

"It is only a whisper now," the man hissed. "But it is coming. It is in your closest friend. Maybe it is in you, too."

That was when a light filled the doorway. In that radiance Duck was surprised to recognize something of himself. In that moment pulsing with a diffused rainbow mist of tenderness whispering, whispering, "Love comes, love comes," Duck was able to pull away and into the night. He felt as if he was surfing on a magic carpet and he thought he heard a voice calling to him, "Do you have a story to tell?"

When he got home Duck looked at his face in the mirror and saw that the bay windows in his eyes had clouded over and there was a roughness about his chin now. What story do I have to tell? Duck wondered.

The next night in his acting class Duck asked Preston Delbert if he could perform a monologue. Preston Delbert looked suspicious.

"I'd forgotten all about you, Duck," he said. "I don't think invisibility and muteness are very good traits for an actor."

"I know," said Duck. "But I have something to say now."

Duck got up in front of the class. His hands felt like they were covered with ice cream. He started to sit back down. Then he heard the voice asking if he had a story to tell. So Duck told the class the story of his mother and father and brothers and sisters. He told the story of Harley and Cherish Marine. And then Duck told the story of Bam-Bam. The class was silent. Some people had tears in their eyes. Duck felt as if his heart was an angel. Bam-Bam's sidewalk angel— that light, that full of light.

Soon Duck will meet his love. When Duck sees his love he will know that the rest of his story has begun. It will not be too late for either of them. The sweetness and openness they were born with will come back when they see each other in the swimming, surfing lights.

And we are still young, Duck will think. I wish I had

met you when I was born, but we are still young pups.

They will still be young enough to do everything either of them has ever dreamed of doing, to feel everything they have always wanted to feel.

When they first kiss, there on the beach, they will kneel at the edge of the Pacific and say a prayer of thanks, sending all the stories of love inside them out in a fleet of bottles all across the oceans of the world.

And the story was over. Dirk felt he had lived it. Was it a story told to him by the man in the turban who now sat watching him from the foot of the bed? Had he dreamed it? Told it to himself? Whatever it was, it was already fading away leaving its warmth and tingle like the sun's rays after a day of surfing, still in the cells when evening comes.

"Who are you?" Dirk asked the man, his voice surfing over the waves of tears in his throat. "Who is Duck?"

"You know who I am, I think. You can call me by a lot of names. Stranger. Devil. Angel. Spirit. Guardian. You can call me Dirk. Genius if I do say so myself. Genie.

"Duck—you'll find out who he is someday."

"Why are you here?"

"Think about the word destroy," the man said. "Do you know what it is? De-story. Destroy. Destory. You see. And restore. That's re-story. Do you know that only two things have been proven to help survivors of the Holocaust? Massage is one. Telling their story is another. Being touched and touching. Telling your story is touching. It sets you free.

"You set some spirits free, Dirk," he went on. "You gave your story. And you have received the story that hasn't happened yet."

Dirk knew he had been given more than that. He was alive. He didn't hate himself now. There was love waiting; love would come.

He was aware, suddenly, of being in a dark tunnel, as if his body was the train full of fathers speeding through space toward a strange and glowing luminescence. He wanted that light more than he had wanted anything in his life. It was like Dirby, brilliant and bracing; it was a poem animating objects, animating his heart, pulling him toward it; it was a huge dazzling theater of love. On the stage that was that light he saw Gazelle in white crystal satin and lace chrysanthemums dancing with the genie, spinning round and round like folds of saltwater taffy. Dirk also saw the slim treelike form of a man in top hat and tails, surrounded with butterflies. When he looked more closely Dirk saw that they were not regular butterflies at all but butterfly wings attached to tiny naked girls who resembled young Fifis. Grandfather Derwood, Dirk thought. And Dirk saw Dirby too, Be-Bop Bo-Peep, tossing into the air wineglasses that became stars while Just Silver, balanced on the skull of death, held up her long ring-flashing hands and moved her head back and forth on her neck. He wanted to go to them. But there was one thing they were all saying to him over and over again.

"Not yet, not your time."

Dirk McDonald saw his Grandma Fifi sitting beside him, her hair cotton-candy pink as the morning sun streamed in on it.

"Grandma," Dirk whispered. He looked around. White walls. The smell of disinfectant. Liquids dripping in tubes, into him.

"Where are we?"

"The hospital," Fifi said. "How do you feel?"

"Better."

"The doctor says you're going to be just fine."

"How long have you been here?"

"Oh, quite some time now. We've been telling each other stories, you and I, Baby Be-Bop. Past present future. Body mind soul," and Grandma Fifi squeezed Dirk's hand, knowing everything, loving him anyway.

Dirk closed his eyes. There was no tunnel but there was light—a sunflower-haired boy riding on waves the ever-changing colors of his irises.

Stories are like genies, Dirk thought. They can carry us into and through our sorrows. Sometimes they burn, sometimes they dance, sometimes they weep, sometimes they sing. Like genies, everyone has one. Like genies, sometimes we forget that we do.

Our stories can set us free, Dirk thought. When we set them free.

Francesca Lia Block

is the acclaimed author of the *Los Angeles Times* best-sellers GUARDING THE MOON: *A Mother's First Year*, THE ROSE AND THE BEAST, VIOLET & CLAIRE, and DANGEROUS ANGELS: *The Weetzie Bat Books*; as well as GOAT GIRLS, WASTELAND, ECHO, I WAS A TEENAGE FAIRY, GIRL GODDESS #9: *Nine Stories*, and THE HANGED MAN. Her work is published around the world.